hamel...n

a

Boy,

and a

Quest

Book 1 of *The Rwendigo Tales*

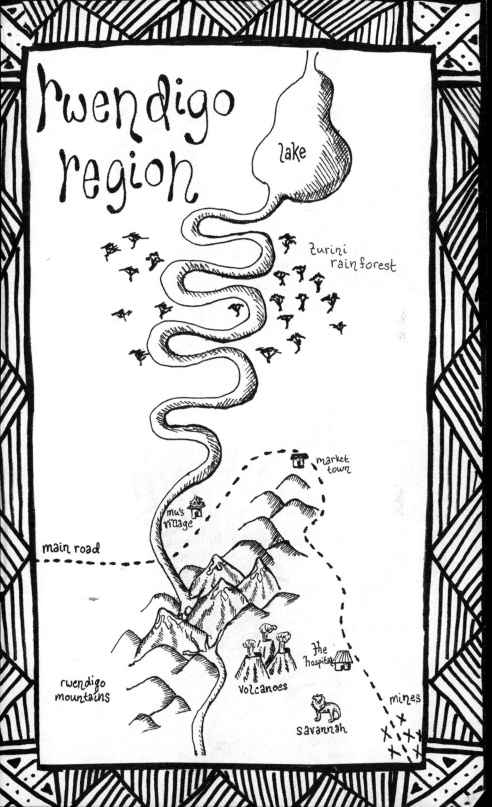

New Growth Press, Greensboro, NC 27404
Copyright © 2015 by J. A. Myhre. All rights reserved.

Published 2015.

Art: Acacia Masso

Cover/Interior Design and Typesetting: Faceout Studio, faceoutstudio.com

ISBN: 978-1-942572-08-4 (Print)
ISBN: 978-1-942572-09-1 (eBook)

Library of Congress Cataloging-in-Publication Data

Myhre, J. A., 1962-
A chameleon, a boy, and a quest / J.A. Myhre.
     pages cm
Summary: Orphaned ten-year-old Mu's drudgery-filled life changes
forever when he meets a talking chameleon and the pair embark on an
adventurous quest in the everchanging landscape of Africa.
ISBN 978-1-942572-08-4 (print) -- ISBN 978-1-942572-09-1 (ebook)
[1. Adventure and adventurers--Fiction. 2. Chameleons--Fiction. 3.
Orphans--Fiction. 4. Africa--Fiction.] I. Title.
PZ7.1.M94Ch 2015
[Fic]--dc23
                         2015016954

Printed in the United States of America

25 24 23 22 21 20   4 5 6 7

A Chameleon, a Boy, and a Quest

Book 1 of The Rwendigo Tales

J. A. Myhre

Illustrated by Acacia Masso

Contents

1. An Unlikely Adventure Begins 1
2. Unexpected Visitors 11
3. A Dangerous Road 20
4. Bandages and a Lullaby 28
5. Stories and Assumptions 35
6. An Escape and a Trek 44
7. A Home of Respite 50
8. Mpali and Hyenas 58
9. Battle at the Anthill 65
10. An Elephant's View 72

11. A Crater and a Cave 79

12. Into the Mountain Forest 86

13. A Cobra, a Bog, and a Cage 90

14. A Courageous Choice 98

15. Child Soldier 104

16. Betrayal 111

17. Redemption 118

18. Toward the Summit 120

19. Through the Pass and Under the Falls . . . 126

20. Journey's End 135

21. The Quest Fulfilled 144

     Epilogue 150

     Glossary 154

     Acknowledgments 159

For Luke, Caleb, Julia, and Jack,

African Adventurers
&
Readers Extraordinaire

*(but mostly Jack on this first book, whose soul is
part-Mu and part-Botu, and because the youngest is always
last and in the Kingdom the last shall be first)*

— CHRISTMAS EVE 2005

Dear Reader,

You are holding a story written for my four children, when
we were living in a spectacularly beautiful but desperately
poor village in the heart of Africa. My Christmas present to
them was this story, which we began on Christmas Eve and
read each evening through the holiday. The characters and
places contain truth, but you will have to decide what really
happened. The story seeks to honor the courage and integrity
of untold thousands of children like Mu, who have little voice
in their lives and sometimes make irrevocable choices along
the path of growing up. I hope you will fall in love with the
people and the place as we have, be thoroughly entertained for
a season as you read, and perhaps open your imagination to
what lies beneath the surface of what we see.

J. A. Myhre

CHAPTER 1

An Unlikely Adventure Begins

The day the chameleon spoke to Mu did not begin with any hint of the extraordinary. Mu woke to the falling trill of a forest kingfisher, followed by the rhythmic coos of the ring-necked dove and finally the raucous twitters of an unruly weaver bird colony. He knew that he should have been heading for the communal water tap sometime between the dove and the weaver birds, but this morning as every other he lay awake staring at the pattern of tiny fissures in the packed mud wall of his house as the lines emerged in the gray light of dawn, seeing yet not seeing, waiting for some pattern to coalesce into a message that made sense of his young life. As usual the language of the lines remained obscure. He tried to ignore the restless movement of his cousins in the narrow bed they shared, and he sighed in resignation when the voice of his great-aunt broke through the weaver bird chatter calling him to get moving.

Sometimes in that moment between sleep and wakefulness, Mu forgot that the hated morning task of water carrying awaited him, forgot the apparent shame of doing what was commonly held to be girls' work. He forgot his worries at school where he had started years late and was therefore the obvious target of many jokes and pranks. He could still feel the warmth of a sympathetic arm on his shoulders for a few seconds . . . until it faded into the world of dreams and memory and left him alone.

Mu rose from the bed, pulled on his shirt and a pair of shorts, reached for the doorway in the dimness of the new day, pushed aside the curtain, and emerged just as the rising sun tinged the clouds pink. He found an empty twenty-liter jerry can just inside the doorway of the cooking hut where he had left it the night before, and then swung it in wide empty arcs as he started down the path toward the piped water his family shared with a half dozen other homesteads in the village. The faded yellow plastic of the container glowed faintly against the black-greens of the thick foliage on either side of the path. He thumped the empty can on its forward arc a few times before thinking better of making such an ominous noise at that hour, though the temporary freedom of the lightness of his burden tempted him to beat out a song. In a few minutes he would be returning with a sloshing weight of water that he could barely drag in a stilted, hopping walk with rests every ten steps. Right now the cool sharpness of the morning, the loneliness of the path, and the absence of the inevitable weight all filled him with a sense of something, a premonition close to joy but tinged with a darker hue, perhaps danger. He felt the slant of the morning sunlight through the palm fronds as a deep ache of the heart, a longing for something he couldn't begin to name. At that precise moment he sensed more than heard a clear voice calling his name, right there on the path, and he stopped abruptly to trace the source of the salutation.

The voice did not come from behind him where his home lay, or ahead where a few girls would be waiting their turns at the tap. The call seemed to come from just over his right shoulder. Mu lifted his eyes to the red leaves of a poinsettia bush; then the small clear voice continued, "Please, Mu, you must be careful how you swing that jerry can, you nearly knocked me right off my branch."

Mu spun around to see who could possibly be playing such an early morning trick on him, at first wildly searching then recovering and trying not to look shamefully frightened or overly startled. He saw no one.

"I'm right here, on this branch. Here, let me darken my color a bit so that you can see me."

As Mu watched, his eyes gradually made out the poised form of a chameleon against the bright green poinsettia stems. Mu stated the obvious, "Chameleons can't talk."

"Ahh, that is where you are wrong. It is humans who can't listen," replied the chameleon. "If we are to be friends let us begin again. I was waiting for you, but when you came swinging that plastic monstrosity I am sorry to say I dispensed with

polite formalities and went straight to the point of saving my skin. Ahem . . . *Olayo*, Mu, how was the night?"

"How was the night?" came Mu's automatic reply, the greeting formula second nature to him as to every other person in the village.

"What's the news?"

"All is peaceful."

"There, that's much better. Ah, where were we, how are those at your home?"

"They are there. And how are those at yours?"

"They are there."

Mu waited, but the chameleon simply blinked and swept his eye around in a jerky circle. Being a child, Mu had already accepted that this remarkable chameleon could indeed talk, had chosen to speak to him of all people, and in fact knew his name. He sensed instinctively that this chameleon was an elder of some sort, a creature with experience who should command respect. So in the role of a child with an adult, he waited. As he watched, the chameleon shot out his sticky tongue and nabbed a sleepy fly that had just landed on the poinsettia flower.

"Excuse me," continued the chameleon, chewing, and gulping. "It's a bit early for us cold-blooded creatures to be up and about, but when I spotted that fly I remembered my hunger, and it is never good to start a journey on an empty stomach."

"Journey?" asked Mu in a baffled voice. "Where are you going?"

"Why, on your quest, of course. I've been sent to announce its beginning."

"Quest? Quest for what? And sent by whom?"

"All that in good time. First I must try not to get you into too much trouble, and if you aren't back soon you'll be missed. Run along and get your water. On the way back, stop for me and I'll ride home on your shoulder. I'm quite adept at making myself difficult to see, so you needn't worry about alarming anyone. I would advise you, for now, not to mention me to anyone." The chameleon rocked back and forth on the stem, mimicking the swaying of the breeze, and then blended so expertly into the foliage that to Mu he seemed to disappear.

Mu ran to the water tap and slapped his jerry can down in the growing line. As he waited, he repeated the entire conversation in his mind. He'd heard strange stories from his uncle, stories of spirits bent on evil, who inhabited snakes and rats and other creeping beings for periods of time to wreak their mischief. Chameleons were especially feared, since it was quite clear to most people that the dramatic changes in the coloration of their skin must be due to the passing inhabitation of ancestral spirits. But Mu did not sense any malicious intent from the chameleon. He made up his mind to pick the chameleon up (he had never actually touched one before) and carry it home on his shoulder.

His conversation with the chameleon had delayed him, so that when he put his jerry can in the line at the tap he was already fourth. He murmured polite greetings to those ahead of him, two sleepy-eyed neighbors who were younger than he and one bossy teenage girl who always made a point of teasing Mu.

"How was the night, Mu?" she asked with false interest.

"Peaceful," Mu mumbled, eyes on the line of jerry cans as he advanced one place.

"You were so late that we thought you weren't coming. In fact we were just discussing that maybe your aunt finally made one of her daughters fetch water so you could sleep later with the boys."

Mu felt the boil of anger begin to seethe in his heart, the laughter of the three girls burning a familiar pain in his chest.

"I'll tell you why I'm late," Mu began, imagining their stunned faces when he took them to see an actual talking chameleon, one that knew his name, no less. But just as he began to explain that he had been chosen for a quest, a small voice reminiscent of the chameleon's echoed in his mind: "I would advise you, for now, not to mention me to anybody." A smudgy cloud of doubt formed. Why shouldn't he tell? Would others be able to hear the chameleon too? Or would he find himself being laughed at as an even greater fool after dragging them along the path searching for a chameleon that could not be found, let alone heard to produce human speech? And what if the whole conversation had been a dream that had crept from his sleep into his waking and walking down the path, a remnant of those nighttime escapes from reality? What if he really was just a ten-year-old boy in the first year of primary school learning the alphabet with a bunch of babies and carrying water with a bunch of girls? What if he had not been singled out for an adventure? Suddenly he became aware that the laughter had stopped, in fact the three girls had left with their containers of water and the school teacher's mother-in-law was telling him to wake up and get out of her way before the water overflowed his jerry can.

Back down the path Mu lurched. He often tied a cloth through the handle of the can and passed it over his forehead to hoist the twenty-kilogram load onto his back, but today he couldn't be bothered to take the extra time, and he hardly noticed the dragging weight. He paused under the poinsettia and set down the dripping jerry can.

There was no chameleon on the branch that overhung the path.

He traced the branch with his eyes, then reached up with his hand to part the veiny red leaves and inspect each stem. No chameleon. Tears welled up in Mu's eyes.

Just as the first sniffle began to break through, he heard his name and saw with relief that the chameleon had picked his way down low on the branch where he rocked, waiting within easy reach.

"Mu, I'm here. From now on you don't have to worry, I won't leave you until you ask me to go."

"Oh, I'll never ask you to go!" Mu exclaimed with feeling.

"Don't be so sure, the future holds many things, and a companion such as I can be a liability in certain situations. Now please do NOT SQUEEZE me, I am still digesting that fly and a small grasshopper. That's it, put me on your shoulder and I shall hold onto your shirt just under the collar here where no one will notice. Off we go."

"What should I call you?" Mu asked as he started off again with a grunt, heaving the water along. He felt he should use a term of respect such as father or uncle or *mzee*, but nothing in his life to that point had given him a clue about the proper terms of respect when addressing a chameleon.

"Ah, names—names and relationship are always an issue with your kind, but my true name will be difficult for you and much too long. You may call me *Tita*, though I do not look like your father or your uncles, I have been sent in a role not unlike theirs."

"I never saw my father, but you certainly are nothing like my great-uncle," Mu giggled, though as he thought of it the coarsely wrinkled skin and darting eyes of his elderly uncle did have a reptilian quality.

"Your name seems a bit odd, my boy. Who gave it to you?" Tita inquired kindly.

"My cousins say that I called myself Mu when I was brought here after my parents died. My great-uncle says it is short for Mubhi, orphaned one. My cousin Nanjula read a book where the main character was named Pi, and she says Mu is another Greek letter, and maybe that means I am someone important."

"Hmmm, very interesting," murmured Tita.

"Tita, will you go to school with me, or should I find you a safe bush before we reach our compound where you can stay until school is over?"

"Mu, there is so much to tell, and events have already been set in motion. I don't know when the Enemy will make his first move. It is best that you keep me with you."

Before Mu could even think of asking who in the world the ominous Enemy was, they had reached the edge of his compound, which now bustled with morning activity. His great-uncle and great-aunt sat on low benches by a smoking fire, poking sticks into the embers to encourage the flames. Most of his cousins were emerging drowsily from their sleeping quarters. Two were arguing over a school uniform shirt that each claimed; his aunt Sylvia stirred porridge over a fire in the kitchen hut, and his other aunt, Alice, was complaining loudly that he came later and later with the water every morning. In short, except for the almost imperceptible weight of the chameleon on his right shoulder, it was like any other morning. Mu smiled to himself as he set down the jerry can of water, and might have looked upon the scene with a trace of nostalgia or tenderness had he known it would be his last morning at home.

CHAPTER 2

Unexpected Visitors

"*Tugende*, **Mu, let's get going**," urged Birungi as he wrapped a piece of roasted cassava in a bright green banana leaf and stuck it in his pocket for a snack. At six, Birungi was always hungry, and always eating his own food and whatever he could charm from his sister and cousins.

Mu was lost in thought, contemplating how the chameleon would hide himself against the garish pink of the school uniform shirt, feeling certain that even a talking chameleon could not achieve that extreme of color. He finished buttoning his shirt and whispered under his breath to Tita, "Hold on, tugende."

Mu and Birungi quickly caught up with their cousin and classmate Zowadi, a quiet, wide-eyed, seven-year-old who seemed to stand on the fringes of the family and the school, ever-observing and rarely speaking. Zowadi walked hand in hand with her twelve-year-old sister, Nanjula, who was in grade five of primary school and could have ignored all three of the grade one students as burdens, but instead shepherded them to school most mornings with stories and proverbs. This morning she had begun a tale of a rabbit and a hyena, but as the boys caught up they begged her to start again. The children walked one and a half kilometers to school each morning, then back again at lunchtime. The older cousins returned for afternoon classes while Mu spent most of his afternoons making sure his three-year-old twin cousins did not get burned in a cooking fire or drown in the river. Girls' work, again, but he hated school so much that he did not complain that he only went half a day.

The morning air still held a trace of coolness as the sun began to burn through the misty clouds. Children trickled into the road like pink petals on a slow current. Nanjula held Zowadi's hand on one side and Birungi's on the other; Mu trailed a few steps behind. Birungi's sister Katusiime made a point of leaving a few minutes earlier or later than the others, so that she could walk with her friends. He could see Katusiime ahead, giggling with the same girls who had teased him at the water tap that morning. They all turned around and looked at him and giggled again, and Mu felt his ears burn with anger. Katusiime was younger than Mu but a full two grades ahead of him in school. Though she was indeed bright, a good student, the gap was not a matter of intelligence but rather the fact that Mu was an orphan whom the family expected to work in return for his food, and only begrudgingly allowed to enroll in school this year. Birungi, Zowadi, and Nanjula somehow

12

sensed the injustice of this arrangement and went out of their way to treat Mu with kindness, but Katusiime sensed instead a threat or competition that she couldn't name. She had always treated Mu with a teasing, needling contempt. However, even her giggles could not dampen Mu's spirits for long on such a glorious morning. With the sun on his back and the important secret of the talking chameleon in his heart, he ignored the stares and skipped to catch up with Nanjula.

At the schoolyard gate the cousins split up to join the rowdy straggling lines of children who formed each grade. Stick-wielding teachers patrolled threateningly, shouting the students into more orderly lines for the national anthem. Mu marched with Birungi, Zowadi, and the other grade one students as they left the central flagpole in front of the school's three classroom buildings to crowd onto wooden benches under the spreading shade of an umbrella tree. With three small, two-roomed brick and *mbati* buildings, it was no surprise to Mu when he began school to find that the six rooms went to the upper grades while the grade one class met outdoors. However, he preferred the distraction of the open air, the stirring of an occasional breeze, the familiarity of wandering goats and pecking hens, and dreaded the idea of moving inside the stuffy, dim, dirt-floored buildings next year.

The last class of the morning was mathematics. The session amounted to little more than the students painstakingly copying simple sums (sums that Mu had known now for years) from the chalkboard propped against the tree trunk into their smudged, folded exercise books. Mu could do this without actually engaging his conscious brain at all, and he had

long finished the ten sums and wandered mentally to reliving the morning's events before he became dimly aware that the teacher had sauntered back from his extended social break with the other teachers and was addressing the class. One by one, the teacher called on pupils to give their answers and then wrote the correct sums by each problem. Almost every class session the teacher called on Mu, hoping to catch him daydreaming, for there was something about Mu's air of patient endurance through the too-easy class that irked his instructor. So when Birungi poked him with a pencil, Mu snapped to attention, quickly realizing that the teacher was asking him to give the answer to one of the sums. Mu stood too abruptly, dropping his book and pencil, which caused the entire class to erupt in laughter. Though this laughter was by no means uncommon when Mu was called upon, at that moment the teacher felt angry that his class was caught looking disorderly just as three very important-looking, heavy-set men in suits arrived at the school gate. He raised his ever-present stick to smack Mu for his impertinence, but paused, stick midair, when he realized at the last second that trailing the unknown visitors was a fourth man, Mu's great-uncle, the *mukumu* himself. The teacher wavered. He suspected that the mukumu would approve of the discipline, and that he would particularly approve of putting Mu in his place. But he wasn't quite sure how the mukumu would react in front of the visitors, and in that moment of hesitation the whole class looked around to see the focus of the teacher's attention, and became very still.

Mu was the last to turn. Since his great-uncle was one of the oldest men in the area's most powerful clan, he often received official visits. And since he was a mukumu, a practitioner of traditional medicine, strangers often came from distant villages to consult him. Mu tried to stay out of the way of these proceedings, which often seemed frightening. He knew his great-uncle embellished all the ceremonies of his trade to impress clients and support his large family, but he also knew that much of what went on in the mukumu's special circular hut smacked of evil. His aunts brushed all fears aside, happy that the consultations generally ended in a good meal for the family as the chickens or even goats proffered as payment were slaughtered. So while it was not surprising to see the mukumu receiving strangers like a king at his court, even important-looking ones in store-bought suits, it was highly unusual to see the powerful mukumu trailing behind strangers who strode confidently ahead—and into the schoolyard no less. The grade-one class shuffled to get a good view, and then stood mutely in amazement. Their low murmur of surprise reached the headmaster within seconds, and before the strangers even had a chance to ask for him, the headmaster materialized, barking orders to older students to bring chairs into his office. With pomp and bustle the visitors were ushered into one of the buildings and out of sight.

Mu sat down, and after a few seconds the class returned to its usual hum of whisper and movement and disorder. Mu frantically snatched his book from the ground and tried to guess which problem he had just been asked to solve, but the teacher forgot all about the sums as he gravitated toward the open shutter of the office in order to hear the mysterious business being conducted.

Left unattended, the students reverted to their usual pastimes of gossip, jokes, stories, and teasing. Mu sketched a chameleon absentmindedly in his exercise book while considering the possible explanations for the arrival of such visitors. An inspection of the facilities by ministry of education delegates from the capital? A marriage dispute involving distant relatives of the headmaster? Businessmen who wished to acquire land in the area? There was no imaginable scenario that would bear the least impact on Mu's life, so he was naturally surprised to see his teacher back in front of the class suddenly, rapping the front row of benches for order, and calling his name, commanding him to come with him.

Mu followed the teacher into the cramped, earth-damp office of the headmaster, where the three men in suits sat uncomfortably in too-small chairs. The mukumu had regained his dignity and was seated in the powerful position behind the desk. The headmaster himself was squeezed into a chair by the door.

"Here he is, the boy of whom we speak, my dear grandson," said the mukumu, falsely elevating the relationship he bore to Mu. "Mu, greet these visitors with proper respect!"

Kneeling on the lumpy dirt floor, Mu bowed his head and murmured humble greetings to each man in turn.

"You can see he is well brought up, as befits a child in my home," boasted the mukumu. "And our headmaster here will testify to his diligence in studies."

Mu had never heard a positive word about himself pass through his great-uncle's lips, and he began to have the uncomfortable sensation that he knew how the cows and goats felt on market day as buyers and sellers haggled over their prices.

The men grunted and murmured together while Mu remained kneeling in front of them. He dared a quick glance up to meet the eye of his great-uncle, but the cold glint of greed he read there frightened him and he looked back down.

"Our final offer is thirty *mitwalos*. After all, we are taking him off your hands, relieving you of the cost of food, clothes, and school fees. It is you who should be paying us!" joked the center man.

"This boy is dear to my heart," sighed the mukumu. "He is the last memory I have of his mother, so I cannot relinquish him lightly." Mu looked up, startled by the believable tone in which his great-uncle could deliver such obvious lies. "But I can see that you gentlemen are offering him an opportunity for advancement, so I must put my personal feelings aside and reluctantly accept your offer. Since you are third cousins of my late wife's brother, I can trust you to care for him even as I myself would."

Even the headmaster had to stifle his laughter at this charade.

"Let us seal the agreement with a meal," concluded the mukumu, rising to signal the end of the negotiation and his intent to return home.

"That will not be necessary," interrupted the center man. Mu was shocked that anyone would dare defy his great-uncle's suggestion. The man was counting out money onto the desk! "We would like to continue our journey so that we can cross the plains before nightfall. He can come with us now," he continued.

At this the headmaster, incredulous, could keep silent no longer. "But the boy has nothing here at school! Surely you will let him go home to gather his clothes, and say a proper farewell to his aunts and cousins."

All eyes turned to the mukumu who, as he pocketed the money, said, "No, we must not keep our visitors waiting. They have important business to the south, and their journey is a long one. I will carry Mu's good-byes to the family, and these uncles will provide whatever clothes are needed when Mu begins his work. There is no need to delay." It was obvious that he was shrewdly avoiding any possibility of a scene at home.

The men shuffled out, blinking as they emerged from the dim office into the bright heat of noontime. From where he still knelt, Mu could see the headmaster framed in the doorway, bowing and shaking hands all around, as the fat men brushed the dust of the chairs from their suits and began walking toward their white pickup truck, which was parked in the shade of a tree along the driveway. No one even looked back at Mu who was shocked into immobility. Had he really just been transferred to the care of these strange men? Had his uncle really taken money for this deal? Was he really leaving the only home he could remember? The thought of Birungi, Zowadi, and Nanjula suddenly crashed into his mind, and a great sob threatened to heave him onto the floor.

"Do not fear," whispered a familiar voice in his ear. "The quest has begun."

CHAPTER 3

A Dangerous Road

Mu crawled up onto a sack of lumpy cocoa beans in the back of the pickup truck. His cousins stared, torn between the desire to wail in protest and their healthy fear of their grandfather, the mukumu, who shook hands with the men in the cab. The engine revved to life with some difficulty, and the driver ground the gears briefly. Mu grabbed onto the rough sacking material, the lumpy contents shifted, and a cloud of dust sifted skyward. The truck bumped out of the school compound and onto the narrow rutted road, covering the kilometer and a half that represented Mu's daily world in only a minute. Mu had seen bigger boys riding expertly on the beds of pickups every market day, swaying on the peaks of impossible mountains of mattresses or clinging to baskets of reeking fish. He had never had the pocket change necessary to ride to town himself, though he had walked the 10 kilometers a handful of times. Watching the lurching trucks from the bushes, Mu had never imagined the actual experience of riding in a *motocah* would be so jarring, nor that the supposed ease of mechanized transport would actually involve the exhausting exercise of holding on for dear life. By the time the truck pulled into town and slowed to a stop in front of the lone pump at the petrol station, Mu's arms were cramped, his teeth gritty, his eyes watering. He did not dare get out of the truck though, unsure of what the men intended. The driver chatted with the station attendant while the others bought sodas and roasted corn.

The chameleon! Mu had almost forgotten, and reached quickly to feel the tiny scaly body of his only thread of hope amidst the bewildering events of the day.

"Don't worry, child," came the reassuring voice in his ear. "Haven't you seen my claws? I can stay on a mango branch in a hailstorm. Even roads this rough and driving this bad can't knock me off."

"Tita," Mu murmured, trying not to be seen talking. "Where are we going?"

"Mu, these are men from the copper mines, and while they are in the habit of coercing children into work, they are certainly not in the habit of paying for them. I suspected that enemy forces might have caught wind of your survival, even as we did. That's why I was sent, to help guide you. We must wait for our chance. In the meantime, a ride south is an unanticipated convenience. So hold on."

The men had moved to a small table shaded by an umbrella, and to Mu's discomfort the driver had started into a substantial brown bottle with a yellow label, the national beer. Well, one beer shouldn't cause too much trouble; he had often seen his uncles down three or four on a night of dancing. Mu decided to take his chances and climb down, but as soon as his feet touched the ground the men were back by the truck, yelling at him to get back up. He climbed onto the rear wheel and reached up to hoist himself into the truck bed, but as his head rose above the cargo he came face-to-face with the powerful snout of a big white dog.

Frightened, Mu jumped down and backed away, his eyes riveted on the fierce dog. One of the men shouted at the dog and made a threatening gesture in an attempt to shoo him off the top of their load, but the dog barked and snarled. The man took a step backward, reached for a stick, then came at the dog again. But the dog stood its ground, grabbing the stick from the man's hands and snapping it in strong jaws. It barked again at the men, then settled back onto the load. The men laughed nervously, by this time joined by the crowd of observers that always seems to materialize in a market for any slightly out of the ordinary event.

"Eyyy, you are fearing that dog!" jeered one onlooker.

"Is it yours? Get it off my truck if you don't want trouble!" retorted the man, trying to sound more confident than he looked.

"That dog belongs to no one here. Last market day it showed up here at the pump. It is well fed and strong, and many shopkeepers have tried to tie it up for nighttime protection from thieves. But that dog is fierce, too fierce."

"Is it dangerous?"

"Who can say? It does not bother anyone unless you try to tie it up. All week it has seemed to be watching the vehicles that come here for petrol, and now it has decided to travel on yours!" the station manager continued, laughing. "My boys are saying it is not a dog at all, but an ancestor looking for a son who has not paid proper respect."

Nervous laughter rippled through the crowd, no one wanting to appear so backward or superstitious as to actually believe such a tale, but no one quite confident that it wasn't true either.

The men looked uncomfortable as the crowd waited to see how they would handle the dog.

"Well," announced the biggest one, "this small boy hardly takes up any room at all. I don't see why this dog can't ride as well. I know some Germans at the mines to the south who keep dogs for guarding their business—they would pay well for an animal like this." He turned to Mu, "Get on, you have delayed us long enough," and moved toward the cab, giving wide berth to the dog.

Mu timidly approached the truck again. He had always feared dogs, even the skinny mongrels that ran in packs through the bush and were easily turned away with a well-thrown stone. The dog did not even raise its head as Mu climbed onto the rear wheel and peeked over the side of the truck bed. The dog easily outweighed Mu, with a yellow-ish-white coat of short thick hair. Mu settled into the very farthest back corner of the truck bed, facing backward, wedging himself between the bags of cocoa beans and bracing

his feet against the side of the truck and the back gate. He glanced again and again to his right to check the dog, imagining that if the creature sprang he would jump out of the truck. But the dog merely looked quietly at him, then sighed a heavy dog sigh and put his head down. The truck coughed to life and soon the jolting and rolling of the road required all Mu's concentration, and he found he could not worry about the dog while worrying about staying aboard the truck.

They followed the district's only exit route, a rutted track that dipped through thick rain forest before skirting the northern shoulder of a mountain range. Mu glimpsed the comical white-bearded cheeks of red-tail monkeys as they swung through high branches of ancient trees, and he felt a pang of envy at their careless freedom. A flock of hornbills quarreled noisily in the fronds of a palm tree, their cackles just audible over the roar of the motor. Soon the road began to climb, and the truck strained up the switchbacks that clung to the side of the mountain. Mu had his first sweeping view of the forested valley in which he had spent his entire life. A textured tapestry of greens stretched far into the distant wavering heat, broken by irregular clearings and the twisting silver coil of a river. The now invisible road that they had traversed was marked by the smoke of cooking fires in villages along its course. The sacks of cocoa shifted until Mu at last reached an equilibrium, gripping the sacking material in one hand and side of the truck in the other, anticipating particularly deep ruts, ducking for low-hanging branches.

An hour passed. Then another. Mu's muscles felt cramped, unaccustomed to the type of pulling and supporting he was forced to do. At first he tried to talk to Tita, but the noise of the engine precluded conversation. His teeth were covered with a gritty film of road dust. Sometimes small *obekekuni* bugs smacked into his nose or eyes if he turned to look ahead. The mountain ridge now loomed to their right as they headed south along the eastern side of the range, into country different than Mu had ever seen. Bright-green banana trees, terraced potato fields, and clusters of mud-walled homes disappeared as the damp humid forest gave way to a dry, grassy plateau. At the rare intersection or petrol station, Mu saw familiar-looking women balancing baskets of tomatoes on their heads, or clusters of idle men playing checkers with bottle caps. But there were fewer and fewer signs of human influence as the road continued south; instead they passed through more open savannah. He remembered Nanjula's lessons on the habitats of their country and the way they had rolled the word savannah around in their mouths, but from the painstaking notes he had helped her memorize he had imagined a flattish valley with bushy, sharp, spear grass, the kind that was cut and dried for roofing, crawling with elephants and lions. Instead he began to see vast, distant plains, land with no end, the limitless open view completely unsettling to a boy accustomed to constricted villages surrounded by rainforest.

The road now was hard and black. Mu supposed this was the improvement called asphalt, put in years ago by the government when the mines and cement factory were important sources of revenue in the newly independent country. But the mines' output had slowed to a trickle, the cement factory produced only enough for local consumption, and the road had not been repaired for a decade. Soon Mu wished for the uniform slow jolts of the dirt road, instead of the lurches of speed and bone-rattling jerks of these potholes. After a while the potholes comprised the majority of the road surface, with occasional bridges of asphalt. Mu stretched his arms a moment as the truck rolled to a near stop for a particularly deep hole. It was just at that moment of slowing, as the nose of the truck dipped into the crater in the road, and Mu's balance teetered, that the dog sprang.

There was no time to think, no time to react, the strangely warm heavy body of the big white dog pushed Mu right over the side of the truck, and everything went black.

CHAPTER 4

Bandages and a Lullaby

"Have you heard anything yet from the village chief, Martha?"

Mu stirred slightly and opened his eyes at the sound of the singsong, high-pitched, foreign voice. Immediately pain shot down the left side of Mu's head and neck, and he closed his eyes again.

"Not yet. I sent the watchman to talk to the police again, and they're trying to trace the registration of the truck. But you know this place, the phones only work half the time, and there is no database. It might be days or weeks before we hear who was in that truck, and by that time no one will care. And, Sister, we don't even know if the boy has any connection to the accident at all." Mu glimpsed through a small slit in his mostly

closed eyelids at the person named Martha, who stood with
her arms folded across a white uniform. She was thin, wrinkled, pale. Mu had never seen anyone like her in his life. Mu
wondered how he could understand the speakers until he realized that the chameleon was translating directly into his ear.

"I have a suspicion that he was on that truck before the accident. I can't explain it but I do. Though I have no explanation for
how he and that dog made it from the highway to our mission—
it's half a kilometer and neither was in any shape to walk."

"I think he's waking up, Mary. Do you suppose he speaks
English? Swahili? Luwendigo?" Martha bent close and tried a
series of greetings, mostly unfamiliar to Mu who was not sure
he wanted to open his eyes again anyway.

"Nothing. Maybe he was on that truck after all, and came
from somewhere far away, up north or out west? We can get
the cook to try and talk to him tomorrow." Martha became
businesslike again. "Whoever he is, what he needs now is
good rest and time. He's young enough that he might recover
completely from the coma; I don't think he has any intracra-
nial bleeding. When he's stable we'll need to get that arm in a
cast. And even if the cook can't get him to talk, maybe he can
get him to eat. He'll never heal without some decent protein."

"You're right, Sister. I think I'll ask the cook to make
chicken with *kahunga* and a good *supu* tomorrow." Mary
patted Mu's leg through the thin sheet.

Martha sighed. "Do not get too attached to this boy, Mary.
In a day or two some angry parents are going to show up here
and beat him for failing to do whatever errand he was being
sent for on that truck. Or a schoolmaster is going to beat him

for running away from school. And then you're going to cry
again, and try to stop the world from being what it is—harsh
and cruel. Let's move on to the next case. I'm hoping the
doctor will be back by Friday for this one."

The voices moved on down the row of beds, and Mu ventured
another peek. He was lying on a low cot in a hospital ward.
Mosquito nets draped like eerie, dingy cobwebs over twenty-
some beds. A flickering bulb lit the ward from the center of the
ceiling, and Mu could see through screened windows that it
was nighttime. In most of the beds mothers lay next to children

who were bandaged or attached to long dripping tubes of fluids hanging from bottles, suspended from makeshift poles or nails in the wall. The two sisters, both dressed in white uniforms with perky white caps and red crosses pinned into gray hair, shuffled down the row from bed to bed, administering last doses of pills or checking drips for the night. They murmured greetings in an almost-understandable local language to each mother, then discussed the cases in their own tongue.

Mu remembered his chameleon, and started to move his right arm until pain told him quickly and certainly that that arm should not be moved a millimeter. Instead he reached up with his left hand and stroked the poky ridge of the chameleon's back.

"Yes, I'm here, though you did your best to crush me," chuckled Tita.

Mu relaxed. His head hurt overwhelmingly, but through the throbbing he could vaguely remember the extraordinary day when he found the chameleon, and was essentially sold to the men in the truck. They were heading south, there was a dog . . . that was it, the dog, the dog that knocked him off the truck must have caused his injuries.

"Oh, Tita, I'm so glad you're here. That dog tried to kill me! How did I get here?" Mu found that as his memories returned he had more and more questions. "Where is this place? How long have we been here? Did they see you? Are the men here too? Will they take me away again? What did she mean about the police?"

"Slow down, my child. Slow down. All in good time. It seems the adventure has truly begun. We have enemies. Some may be right here—the sisters are on our side but even they have a few rats and roaches that frequent the ward at night and could take tales back to interested ears."

"Whose ears? Who is this enemy? Is it one of the men in the truck?"

"No, the men in the truck were not good men, but they were unwittingly part of the Enemy's plan. The real enemy is Abaddon. Have you never heard his name before?"

"Abaddon . . ." Mu pondered. "No, it does not sound like any name I have ever heard. Is he from our country, or some other?"

"That is the name that men used for him when this world was younger. It means the Destroyer. Deception and destruction are his main goals, for he sets himself against truth and beauty even though he often cleverly disguises himself. We will not talk much of him. It should not surprise you, from the little you have seen of life, to know that the forces of evil continuously encroach upon all creation. Your struggle will be against those who work for Abaddon. But enough of that for tonight. These are not good things to speak of in the darkness. You must sleep. I will explain more tomorrow when it is light."

"Sleep? How could I possibly sleep . . ." Mu began to say, but he felt overwhelmingly tired, and suddenly the realization that he was in a real bed with a real mattress for the first time in his life, sharing with no one other than a very small chameleon, made him feel grown up. And a little lonely. Tears came to his eyes as he thought of his cousins.

"I am going to sing you a lullaby. It's about a baby and a dragon and stars and swords. We like to sing this story where I come from. Close your eyes and listen."

And before Mu could wonder how a chameleon could sing, the most beautiful melody he had ever heard filled his ears, and behind his closed eyes he saw fantastic visions of a dragon's tail sweeping stars from the sky, of a baby in danger being snatched up in the arms of a shining and muscular black warrior, and of a tender mother kissing him good-bye.

CHAPTER 5

Stories and Assumptions

And so began an almost idyllic month. If a month in an obscure rural health center with a concussion and a broken arm can be described as idyllic, then the desperation of Mu's short life becomes quickly apparent. Sister Mary and Sister Martha treated him with a care and deference he had never before experienced from the hands of an adult. They puzzled over his origins, but as they grew used to his presence they began to worry less about their inability to trace any family and more that a family would come and snatch the boy back.

Mu looked for opportunities to consult with Tita, though avoiding listening ears proved difficult. His long visits to the latrine were assumed to be an adjustment of his intestines to the trauma and recovery, but in fact were rare moments of privacy where Tita could gorge on flies between answering questions. In this way Mu learned a bit about his parents, about whom his great-uncle's family never spoke. Tita's story, pieced together over the weeks, went like this:

Mu's father, Mugisa, was a medical doctor, from a valley over the mountains. He had come to the Rwendigo area when an outbreak of a mysteriously fatal disease proved to be Ebola, and most medical workers had either fled or died.

The area had only two other doctors in the best of times, and both were unavailable attending a seminar (so they claimed) in the capital. So the people eagerly welcomed the new doctor. Being a wise man, Mugisa immediately enlisted the help of traditional birth attendants and even healers of sorts, the old women and men respected in the villages. While he was administering his herbs and fluids to patients in the hospital, he sent these elders into all the villages to stop the spread of the disease. They forbade the killing and eating of monkeys, demonstrated hand-washing and isolation techniques, and sought out potential cases and brought them for treatment. Within a month the spread of the virus had been arrested. Of the several hundred infected persons treated at the hospital, less than a dozen died after Mugisa began to work, mostly those who had come in advanced stages.

Because the rest of the country feared this epidemic, word of the mysterious doctor and the miraculous cures did not spread beyond the mountain range to the east or the river to the west for many months. Mugisa stayed on, working, healing, teaching. But in those few months something else was happening. The oldest and most powerful mukumu in the whole region had participated at first in the public health campaign. *Mugisa visited his compound often, and there he fell in love with the mukumu's niece Zebiya. Zebiya cooked him delightful meals, listened to his stories, rejoiced over every cure, and cried with him when patients were lost. As Zebiya and Mugisa's friendship grew, the mukumu's suspicion, jealousy, and then hate also grew. His heart had long been in the grip of Abaddon, who now turned it to his own evil purposes. The mukumu began to question Mugisa's qualifications and origins. He stirred up the government administrators and the newly returned doctors, who resented Mugisa's popularity with the people.*

The day that Mugisa came to ask for Zebiya to be promised to him in marriage, the old mukumu was waiting with the police. Mugisa was arrested and went willingly to jail, where he escaped with ease that night when the jailors all got drunk. He came in secret to Zebiya and asked her to leave with him. They went to a faithful priest and were married at dawn the next morning. Mugisa decided that Zebiya was not yet ready to leave her people completely, and that the best thing would be for them to live nearby for a year and try to mend relations before he took her back to his home.

Being a strong man and very much in love, Mugisa cleared a homestead in the Turini Forest and taught Zebiya how to live off of the native plants and animals. For many months they were happy, growing in oneness. Zebiya sent messages to her uncle through trusted intermediaries, hoping for reconciliation. None was offered, and she feared Mugisa's arrest if they returned. Before the year was over Zebiya became pregnant. When the mukumu learned of this, the tone of his replies changed. He opened the door to a potential meeting after the baby's birth. Mugisa attended his wife's labor, and assisted

*her in delivering a baby boy. She was a mother so full of joy
and goodness that she could not imagine anyone resisting her
love. Though Mugisa had doubts, they invited her family for
the traditional ceremony at four days of age when the umbil-
ical cord falls off and the baby is named. The mukumu came
to the house in the forest with his entourage of wives and children. There was a great feast.*

*Thus began eighteen months of an uneasy truce. Mugisa
sensed the mukumu's apparent appeasement was merely a
front for his planned revenge, but Zebiya so longed for the
fellowship of her family and the blessings of her uncle that
her good faith for a while sufficed to keep relations cordial.
Mugisa delayed his return to his own home until he could
rest assured that Zebiya had recovered strength enough for
the journey, and that the baby would not be made ill by the
altitude in crossing the mountains. They began making plans
to travel during the next dry season. Though Zebiya worried
over leaving her family, she was eager to see at last the place
that Mugisa spoke of, and meet his parents. Mugisa warned
her to keep their departure a secret until the last day, but
either Zebiya let hints of their coming journey slip into conversation, or spies of the mukumu had penetrated the forest.
Because the night before their departure, there was an attack
on Mugisa and Zebiya's home. There were men, guns, and
chaos. In the end the baby was brought to the mukumu's house
as an orphan, the demise of his parents blamed conveniently
on a cross-border attack by rebels who periodically launched
incursions from across the western river border.*

Mu collected this story in bits and pieces over the first month
of his recovery. He sensed that Tita carefully dispensed

information as it was requested, rather than pushing any particular agenda. While schoolwork had always been a matter of force-feeding, Mu found that Tita's technique pushed him to ponder. Key bits of his story still eluded him, but he could not seem to find the right questions to unlock the full picture.

The hospital staff spoke a dialect that Mu quickly picked up due to its similarity to his own tongue. For the first two weeks he did not speak at all to any humans, or even respond to questions, but listened carefully. This encouraged the staff to speak freely around him, assuming he could not understand. In this manner he learned that the truck he had been riding on had hit a deep pothole in the tarmac only moments after the dog knocked him off. The driver had lost control, the truck flipped and rolled, the extra fuel ignited, and none of the occupants survived.

It was only after gathering these facts that Mu was willing to listen to Tita about the dog.

"Do not be quick to judge any living creature, Mu. Many who were created for goodness appear frightening in the presence of evil. You need not fear this dog," Tita would insist when Mu was well enough to sit in his bed and glimpsed the dog lying outside in the courtyard. But though Mu remembered little of the accident day, he could replay endlessly in his mind the fearful moment when the dog had lunged at him in the back of the truck. He felt more than remembered the terror of having to climb into the back of the truck with the monstrous, stubborn, snarling beast. For many days, he could not bring himself to listen to Tita's calm reasoning.

Mu could see that the dog limped badly at first, though it seemed to recover more quickly than he did. Once he overheard the staff laughing that Sister Mary and Sister Martha, who had fenced the hospital compound to improve the hygienic nature of the surroundings, keeping out all forms of animal life, now allowed an unknown wounded dog to rule the territory. The dog never disturbed the cooking pots patients' families tended in the courtyard. When the cook brought patients their daily ration of porridge in the morning or beans and *posho* in the evenings, Mu noticed that a bowl was always filled for the dog. It seemed quite content to guard the ward, accept the cook's provisions augmented by a daily array of scraps from the patients themselves, and rest and heal.

One day Tita asked him, "Have you yet wondered, my child, why you were not killed on that truck?"

Mu sighed uncomfortably. The thought had begun to trouble him. "Tita, I suppose that someone had cursed those men, and I am prepared to believe they deserved it. The curse did not include me because I joined them late." Even as he said the words, Mu knew that they were an inadequate explanation. His life in the compound had made him see the world as a series of curses and escapes from curses, both of which generally involved a substantial income for his great-uncle. Now in the hospital, he wondered for the first time about that. Many, many patients came through, and he had a hard time imagining how many *mukumus* would have to be around the place to keep up such a steady stream of sickness and injury. And a good number of the patients recovered with none of the ceremonies that Mu was accustomed to witnessing. Certainly the mechanisms of healing in the ward were equally mysterious with tiny bags of pills or intravenous fluids, but no chanting or sacrifice was evident. Tita's reply pulled him back from this disturbing new line of thought.

"And if you were not to be cursed, how did you come to separate yourself from those who were?" Tita pressed. He had elected to skip right over the whole question of curses and stick to the practicalities of what actually happened.

"I, I guess I jumped off the truck at just the right time?" Mu offered.

Tita remained silent.

"Well, maybe I didn't exactly jump. Are you telling me the dog pushed me off? That the creature's attempt to kill me ended up saving my life?"

Tita was still silent. Yet again, Mu replayed the terrible moment when the dog jumped up and pushed him off. For the first time he realized the dog had not bitten him after all. And he faintly remembered feeling the body of the dog somehow beneath him as they hit the embankment on the roadside and rolled and rolled.

"Are you telling me the dog was not trying to kill me but save me?" Mu drew a deep breath. His life had consisted of endurance, of trying to stay out of the way, out of trouble. He had been made to feel that the fact he had food to eat and a mat of banana leaves on which to sleep was a great miracle of kindness afforded his unworthy parentless self by his overtaxed relatives. When his great-uncle ordered him into the truck with the men of dubious purpose, when he awoke in a strange hospital with injuries, it seemed to be just two more realities that he had to learn to endure. Now Tita was gently reminding him that perhaps he had been chosen for some purpose, that his life had been intentionally spared.

"But Tita, who would know me, who would care about me? I'm not anyone." Mu truly believed that. "I never even heard of this enemy Abaddon until now. What could I possibly have to do with any struggles between good and evil? Maybe my father was that kind of person, but not me. What are you trying to say?"

"I am not trying to say anything, I am simply asking you to think logically about what has happened. And logic would suggest that you might be wrong in your assumptions about the dog; and that you might have some reason to be thankful, and someone to whom you should express that thanks."

Mu might have thought about this for many hours while sitting on the veranda of the hospital ward. But at that moment he became aware of voices, voices that were much louder than usual. And he wasn't the only one, the more mobile patients and their caretakers were edging toward the small office building by the front gate from which the voices emanated. As Mu watched, three men in police uniforms emerged with Sister Mary. He caught a few snips of conversation through the gathering crowd: "was a runaway from the mine school, yes, the family wants him sent back . . ." and Sister Mary's countering "but you must show me some documentation, this is not properly stamped . . ." Mu sensed the controlled panic in her voice and wondered whom the disturbance was about.

Suddenly the big dog barked. It was the first time Mu had heard him make a sound since the day of the accident. He barked and barked, angrily, advancing toward the police. The policemen drew up short and one raised a threatening club. Now the crowd started to back away, screening Mu from view. At that instant, Tita commanded: "RUN!"

CHAPTER 6

An Escape and a Trek

The hospital compound had only one main gate, in the front, directly behind the gathering crowd and the threatening policemen. But Mu had watched the cook take *matoke* peelings and empty salt bags to a deep trash pit in the back corner of the property, and seen how local children had pulled loose a section of the fence to explore the pit for any discarded treasures. He instinctively slipped around the corner of the ward and then ran for the bushy corner near the pit. Taking care not to fall in, he slipped easily under the fence. Once through the fence, he crawled through the elephant grass, keeping his head below the top of the stalks so that his passing would look like nothing more than a rippling breeze. The sharp blades of the tall grass scratched his arms and neck.

A few meters into the grass he became aware that the sound of the barking had stopped, but he continued to push through the grass for a few more minutes.

"Climb that tree," Tita whispered. "We must wait for him."

"For whom?" grunted Mu as he found a decent foothold to hoist himself up the mango tree. He found a spot where he could rest on a strong branch but be well hidden by the dark green leaves, and even managed to pocket an overlooked semi-ripe mango from the tree, which was usually picked clean by the same children who scavenged in the trash pit.

The chameleon did not answer. For the moment, his interest was focused on the well-fed mango flies.

Through the screen of leaves Mu could make out the hospital compound, though he was now too far away to hear any words. The knot of commotion emerged from the back of the ward building, policemen in the middle gesticulating and Sisters Mary and Martha raising their palms in protestations of innocence. By now Mu understood that the policemen were looking for him, though the Sisters were unable to explain his absence. His relief in escaping was tinged by guilt at the thought of the Sisters, who had shown him great kindness and healing mercies, should be blamed.

"They do not know the true story of events, so there is really no blame that can be assigned," assured the chameleon, who often seemed to intuit Mu's thoughts. "Though they are mostly unaware of the true forces against which they fight, the Sisters do much good by their cheerfulness and service."

"Who are those men, and why are they looking for me?" asked Mu.

"I see now that I let you stay at the hospital too long. I was counting on the fact that everyone in the truck was assumed to have been killed, and that you needed much rest before the next part of our journey. It would have been better for us to have left with provisions for you, for crossing the savannah will not be easy. But it's too late now, we can't go back. We will wait for nightfall, and the arrival of Botu, and then set out."

"Botu? Who is that? In my language that means friend, but you're my only friend."

"Friend, yes, a weak word in current usage, but Botu is truly your protector and loyal companion, so you could say friend. I mean the dog, of course."

The dog . . . His thoughts toward the dog had begun to change, but it was difficult not to feel some dread at his coming. Still, as Tita had challenged, thinking logically he had to admit that on the truck Botu's presence and well-timed leap had saved his life. Even the barking a few minutes ago had created the opportunity for escape. He watched the men search the compound, looking into the small surgical theatre, the staff houses, the office, even the latrines. After an hour he could see the dust rise from the far side of the compound and extend eastward along the road, signaling that the men had left. Patient life seemed to return to normal in the compound. Mothers squatted by their cooking fires or scrubbed cloths near the water tap, laying the fading cottons over bushes to dry in the afternoon sun. Siblings chased each other or played football, kicking around a tied wad of banana leaves. Patients lay on mats in the shade. The cook stirred a large pot of posho porridge enriched with milk and oil, which the sisters insisted all the pediatric patients drink for afternoon tea. He finally saw Sister Mary and Sister Martha emerge from the ward and go into their office to take their own tea. Both were slightly bent over, downcast, moving slowly. Mu felt a pang as he realized he would be leaving them, and dared to hope that their dejection might indicate that they also felt some sadness at his disappearance.

He slipped back down to the shaded ground under the tree, and slept.

When the cool, wet nose of Botu nudged him awake, he jumped, startled by the depth of his sleep, the quickly deepening dusk, and the proximity of the once-feared dog.

But chuckling with obvious delight, Tita said, "Botu, my friend, you have done well indeed. May the cook live a long and prosperous life with a hundred grandchildren for this kindness!"

In Botu's mouth was a small basket, the type that people in this area wove from the rushes of papyrus that grew near the lakes to the south and east. They used a design such that a removable lid was connected to the long basket by two straps that could be used for carrying. Inside Mu saw that the cook had filled two discarded IV fluid bottles with clear drinkable water, and wrapped several portions of thick posho in banana leaves. There was even an old medicine tin full of stew.

"My food is ever pestering us, and Botu can fend for himself quite well, but this will make the care of the human boy much easier for the first day or two," muttered Tita. Then to Mu he commanded: "Eat, but not too much. This must last until we are in a safer place. The moon rises in half an hour, and we must be off."

And so began Mu's trek across the savannah. That night they left the last outposts of villages behind, heading due south from the hospital and then bearing slightly southwest. Mu carried the basket on his back and used a smooth walking stick to steady his way. Tita rode as always on his shoulder, and Botu trotted a few paces ahead, choosing the path. Now that Mu's fear had lessened, he ventured during their first rest to touch the dog, tentatively. Botu allowed himself to be stroked, and even gave one encouraging thump of his tail. Mu could tell that Tita and Botu communicated with each other frequently, discussing footpaths, confirming navigation by various star formations. The moon dimmed only a ring of stars as it crossed the night sky, in every other direction the heavens sparkled ever brighter as they left all human lights far behind. Mu was used to the darkness and quiet of the African night, but always a small *kadobba* paraffin lamp had been at hand. Now they walked by the light of moon and stars only. As the night wore on, the paths became more crossed, more frequent, and more confusing. This puzzled Mu since he could see no other sign of villages or human passing at all.

"These are not the paths of men!" laughed Tita, sensing his question as usual. "You will not see men now for many days, at least I hope not. These are the paths of the hippo, the buffalo, the kob, and the waterbuck. They are not made for journeys, but to move from grass to grass and water hole to water hole. But if any creature can find a direction through these mazes, it is Botu. Fear not."

And Mu later remembered that those words, *Fear not,* brought him unaccountable comfort in spite of the apparent facts of his situation: he had been sold by his own great-uncle whom he now knew was likely to blame for the fact he was an orphan to begin with; he was barely recovered from a broken arm and serious concussion; men in police uniforms sought him; and the specter of a nebulous enemy named Abaddon hung over him. What's more, walking in the dark through a territory populated by wild animals, he had no gun, no light, no map, and no help other than a mysterious dog and a tiny chameleon. He did not know where he was going, yet he had nowhere better to turn back to. Still, he began to sense the truth in the words: Fear not.

CHAPTER 7

A Home of Respite

Mu's head nodded forward even as his feet stumbled. The deepest darkness was now fading into the first hints of dawn, accompanied by a slight breeze and the first rustling, uncertain notes of the hornbill.

"Only a few hundred meters more, Mu, stay with us, stay awake, we are almost there."

Mu looked around. He could begin to make out the outline of anthills, scattered acacia trees, clumps of vine-covered cactus. The barely discernible path marked by buffalo hooves wound around the nearest anthill; indistinguishable from any other path he had been walking for the last six hours.

"Almost where? I don't see anything!" mumbled Mu.

At that very moment Botu drew up beside a nondescript hole in the ground beneath an acacia tree, and gave a short bark.

They halted, expectant, though what they were expecting Mu could not guess. Botu barked again, and within moments a round gray muzzle, blotched with the orange-red of the clay bank, appeared sniffing from the hole. Then scruffy whiskers, two worn tusks, flattened ears, and a bristling body on stubby legs emerged with much grunting from the narrow opening. Though Mu had lived his entire life in the heart of Africa, he had only heard of most of the continent's famous wildlife from stories or sketches in school books. His village was surrounded by other villages and the larger animals had long ago migrated away from the dangers of the ever encroaching gardens with their possessive owners. So when this animal began to emerge from the ground, Mu slowly stepped back, torn between curiosity and a healthy fear of the tusks and jaw.

Botu barked short, intelligent, meaningful sequences, which were answered by a staccato of grunts from the warthog. The warthog glanced repeatedly at Mu during this exchange. Tita began to explain.

"You cannot hear them, because the hearing of the language of the universe has been lost to your race after men turned to evil. This warthog is no ordinary warthog; she is Ngiri. She and her brave husband are our allies here on the savannah. Botu has explained your situation and suggested that you take shelter in Ngiri's hole during the heat of the daylight hours. Ngiri is replying that the hospitality of the warthog has never been questioned. She and her children spend most of the day out of the hole grazing, so you are welcome to rest inside. Now Botu is enquiring after her husband, since she did not yet mention him."

Tita paused. Though Mu could not understand the form of language passing between the dog and the warthog, he could tell that the news was not good.

"What? What are they saying?"

Tita sighed. "Not now, Mu, not now. When you are ready I will tell you."

The somber mood was dispelled suddenly by the appearance of a miniature version of Ngiri—one, then two, then three warthog piglets climbed out of the hole to stand behind their mother. Like Mu they seemed curious but fearful, noses quivering as they tried to sort out the strange scent and appearance of Botu and Mu.

Ngiri grunted quietly, then headed off down the trail at a slow trot. The three piglets immediately fell into line behind her; tails erect, heads up, the line of warthogs slipped away into the grassland. At Tita's instruction Mu then climbed down into the hole to find a cool den scraped out of the clay. Though the sun was just appearing, Mu realized the air temperature was rising rapidly, so the dark quiet of the underground dwelling came as a relief. Once through the opening, he found the space large enough for sitting, turning around, and lying on his side. Botu followed, blocking the hazy light from entering the hole, turned, then lay down with his head just below the entrance, as if on guard. Mu tentatively draped his arm over Botu's flank, a gesture that stirred some memory in his heart of sleeping nestled into a safe, warm body. That memory was like the dreams that always eluded Mu when he awoke . . .

When he did wake up, he was alone in the hole. The entrance was now blazingly bright to his sleepy eyes. He rubbed them

and crawled out, giving his sight a moment to adjust to the blinding light. He was just wondering where Botu had gone, feeling a bit vulnerable without the dog's presence, when Tita began to talk.

"Ah, a bit of sunlight, thank you. I've been wanting to wake you for the last hour, but the drawback of the reptilian life is that a cold dark hole slows us down so severely that you could neither hear my voice nor feel my prods. Yes, now my energy is returning. Botu needs less rest than you; he is out scouting. He left Ngiri on watch."

As Mu cleared the hole and sat under the acacia tree, he saw now that Ngiri and her three children were kneeling nearby, their front legs bent to bring their mouths closer to the ground as if praying. They munched the sparse grass near their home, eyes darting in every direction on guard against danger.

Mu leaned back against the tree and reached into the basket to finish the stew from the night before, and a second bundle of posho. The water was now more than half gone, and he realized that in this heat he would need more soon. He dipped his finger in and let a drop collect on the tip, which Tita could then lap up with his sticky tongue.

"Put me down right over there by those buffalo droppings, I shall have a feast," instructed Tita happily. "Nothing like a bit of spoor in the afternoon sun for attracting a chameleon's banquet."

While Tita fed, Mu noticed one of the piglets edging closer and closer as he grazed. He would crawl forward on his elbows, rear end still up in the air, crunching the dry tough roots of grass, eyes intent on Mu. Whenever their eyes met, the young warthog would look back down, pretending to be merely searching for grass. After about fifteen minutes of this game the piglet was near enough for Mu to touch. He sat very still, pretending not to notice the young animal. Almost imperceptibly Mu began to inch his hand out toward the young warthog. Immediately it darted toward Ngiri, tail up, a clatter of little hooves in the dust. The two siblings, taking the warning seriously, dashed to positions of safety behind their mother.

Mu laughed, a hearty belly laugh that further frightened the skittish warthogs. After a quick check around the clearing, Ngiri realized the source of the alarm, grunted assurance to her children, then relaxed and resumed her watchful munching. Mu suddenly remembered Tita, and quickly reached over to pick him up again.

"Next time you start a stampede, please be sure I am safely out of the way first!" exclaimed an indignant Tita. "The savannah is full of dangers for a young warthog, so their survival depends on caution. Run first, question later. You might do well to take a few lessons from Ngiri on living in the wild."

"I'm not afraid," declared Mu, forgetting the sounds of the night, the loneliness of the sky, now in the bright ordinariness of solid earth.

"Well, perhaps you should be," muttered Tita.

"I killed a snake once in my uncle's compound," Mu said confidently. "My cousin ululated the alarm, and I had been working in the garden with a hoe. I was the first to reach him, and my strike caught the mamba just behind the head." Mu neglected to mention that the snake was a baby, barely bigger than an earthworm, wiggling in the dust. Nor did he mention that the men had uncovered the lightning-fast mother snake later that afternoon behind some cooking pots and had surrounded her armed with sticks and *pangas* while Mu perched on the wall of the *kitubbi* seeking safety.

"Most of the animals here will not take much note of you, except to hide or run," Tita said. "Unless you foolishly threaten them or their children, they will go by their code of live and let live. But there are a few of which I must warn you. You are not in the village anymore; the snakes here are not like the worm of your victory." Here Mu felt shame and hung his head. "The buffalo is powerful and dangerous, but only if provoked, likewise the hippopotamus, elephant, and giraffe. All of these are large and thus easily seen and avoided. All would rather avoid contact with you, and you will be wise to do the same. If we encounter these animals, we will back away or quietly climb a tree or enter a hole until they pass.

"The small, insidious dangers are the ones that must keep us alert. When you walk and sit, move stones, or climb trees, watch for the scorpion, the snake, and the *mpali*, the stinging ants. We have no friends among those three species.

"Likewise the hyenas and the baboons have become our enemies. The former hunt by night. The latter may appear in the daytime, seeming harmless enough with their loud, rude, curious banter. But take my word that they are to be avoided; they sport with death and have thrown off the law of the savannah."

Here Tita paused. The bush had seemed benignly attractive a few moments ago, the domestic tranquility of the feeding warthogs almost homelike in quality, the buzz of cicadas and bees displaying a comforting natural indifference to

Mu's presence. Brilliant orange and turquoise butterflies had landed near Tita's lunch spot. All seemed in order. Yet as Tita spoke, a cloud passed over the sun. Mu suddenly caught a whiff of danger in the midst of this beauty.

"We will move carefully. Botu will not allow us to stumble unaware into danger, and we have our allies. I do not want fear to paralyze you, but overconfidence is also unwarranted," Tita concluded in a gentle voice.

When Botu returned, he, Tita, and Ngiri held whispered consultations that were not translated. To pass the time, Mu squatted in the shade, playing a solitary game with a handful of rocks, scattering them and then snatching them up while tossing one in the air. He was so preoccupied that he did not even try to catch the tone of the conversation until Tita informed him that it was time to rest in the hole again while Ngiri and her family napped in the shade. Later in the day Botu would take them to a fresh water spring he had located.

What would Birungi, Zowadi, or Nanjula think of me now, wondered Mu as he tried in vain to sleep again in the warthog den. He was surprised to realize how little he had thought of the only home he had known since leaving it, but the events that bore him along occupied him fully. Like most children, Mu had a natural capacity to accept the present moment as normal, without too much reflection on what might have been. Yet the three warthogs clustering around their mother somehow stirred homesickness in Mu's young heart. In spite of the difficulties of his former life, he found himself missing his cousins, and a small tear trickled down his cheek before sleep finally overtook his grief.

CHAPTER 8

Mpali and Hyenas

Mu saw himself in a basket like the one Botu had brought food in, but much larger. He was covered with bright *kitengi* cloth, and there was something warm near him. He reached out his hand and found that the warmth came from a puppy, which licked his finger. Just as he giggled, he heard a shout and the basket was upturned; he heard angry voices; then he was falling... He awoke, blinking, trying to recall the dream as he became aware that Botu was licking his hand to wake him up.

"Time to go for water," Tita reminded him. This of course made Mu inordinately thirsty. He took a long drink from his remaining bottle when he crawled out, but refrained from emptying it in case the search for water proved long.

As Mu stretched and began to follow Botu down one of the faint trails, he glanced back to see the warthogs reclaim their hole. The three piglets trotted happily inside, followed by Ngiri, who backed into the hole protecting them for the night. Frogs began a raucous disturbance nearby, and Mu realized that the line of trees and bush to the left, slightly south of their westward path, followed a river. Tita explained that the river water was not optimal; since many animals used it for bathing, it would not be clean enough for an unaccustomed human to drink. But that morning he had found a clean spring which fed into the sluggish river, and that was where he was leading them now.

The sun sank rapidly in front of them, until it rested on a shadowy ridge of mountains in the distance. The dust in the air produced a diffuse orange effect, unlike the cloudy pink Mu often saw in the wetter jungle on his side of the mountains. Suddenly he realized that the mountains toward the sunset were likely the same range he used to see at sunrise, and here he was on his way to get water at the junction of night and day. The continuity gave him comfort as the trees and mounds became more indistinct in the twilight.

Suddenly Mu felt a stinging, painful jab on his ankle, then another on the other leg up near his knee. He came quickly out of his thoughts to hear Tita hiss, "Aieeee! I was trying to tell you Botu warned you to jump over that line of mpali, and you were so lost in the sunset that you stepped directly into their path. Aieeee! Quickly strip off your clothes and pick those ants off your body before they reach me!"

Mu did not need to be told twice; mpali were one danger he was familiar with. He dashed ahead to a clear spot, tore off his clothes, and picked ant after ant off his legs and back. These were large, fierce ants with sharp pincers. Once they met resistance they locked onto their victim. Drops of blood appeared on his skin where he removed them. Slowly the full danger of what was happening dawned on him: first, these ants, merely a nuisance to him, would be deadly to Tita. Second, walking through the wild at night with open wounds and fresh blood on his body would not be a good idea. There were hyenas, even lions. Tita had not mentioned the lions, though Mu was sure he had heard a coughing call he imagined to be theirs the night before. He shuddered.

They continued on the trail, Mu now carefully watching where he put his feet, though the diminishing light would barely enable him to distinguish another dark column of mpali from a crevice in the cracked earth, or a stick across the path. Within minutes Botu turned aside and led them to scramble over some rocks. Mu heard the trickling sound of water, and there between the boulders he saw a spring bubbling. Thankfully, he bent over to drink, splashing his face and washing his hands then cupping them to bring the cool water to his mouth. Dipping his finger in the stream, he held it above Tita's head to let a drop form on the tip, and as the chameleon reached his tongue up to take the drop, Mu felt pleasure in Tita's accepting swallow. He rinsed and refilled both IV bottles, then sat back on the rocks to eat the last portion of posho. Guiltily he then thought to offer some to Botu, who was now drinking from the stream. But Botu shook his head, and Tita confided that Botu had caught his own meal midday, not to worry. In fact their next stop would be a tree where Botu had located honey and negotiated with the bee colony there to share it with Mu. They showed him how to pick a dry, oblong, bread-like fruit, break it open, then dip it in the honey for a reasonably tasty meal.

Thus fortified, Mu was ready to return to the warthog hole, but Tita told him they must move on.

"I didn't even say good-bye." Mu had spent only one day with Ngiri and her family, but he felt reluctant to move on into even more unknown territory.

"She knows your gratefulness, words are often unnecessary with us animals."

Certainly Tita seemed to sense Mu's thoughts and attitudes, so he would have to be content with the assurance that the warthog family was similarly aware. Again Mu thought of his cousins and home—though objectively he had not been treated as a son, it was the only home he had known. He had, over the years, come to believe that his state of affairs was the only one possible for him, that there was some inherent defect in his person that determined his lot as servant, scapegoat, last in line, not-quite-member of the large household.

"Tita, does Ngiri raise those young ones alone? I thought warthogs maintained pairings for life, at least I think I heard that in school once." The reality of the animals that were the subject of his learn-to-read books now occurred to him.

"Ah, that is a sad story and not one to be told in the dark to small boys."

Mu did not find this enigmatic reply very comforting.

Though the moon's cycle was now slightly past full, their stop at the honey tree had given time for the faded daylight to be replaced by the rising moon, large and crisp on the eastern horizon in its rapid equatorial ascent. Mu found that once again Botu seemed familiar with the paths, occasionally pausing to sniff one branch or the other but never showing hesitation over their direction. They walked on quietly. Rumbling snorts of hippos emanated from the direction of the river as the gray shapes emerged from the water to graze on grasses for the night, their bulk improbably supported on stubby legs. An occasional nightjar sang from its nesting spot on the ground as they passed. Stars appeared in the nighttime splendor that only an African plain can provide, undimmed by even a candle's glow, a dusting of diamonds above their heads.

Their general direction followed the river westward, toward the distant ridge of mountains. Just as Mu began to wonder if they would walk the entire night, Botu stopped and Tita announced a rest period. The dog circled an abandoned anthill, sniffing carefully as he checked for snakes. Finally, satisfied with the spot, he lay down beside it. Mu sat and leaned against the red clay mound. The moon was now overhead, so Mu guessed it was past midnight. Tita cautioned him that they would rest for an hour at most, but then they must continue. Mu had never expected too much comfort in his sleeping places and the exhaustion of the last two days of walking soon overtook him.

He awoke, dimly aware of a low vibrating growl from Botu. Immediately adrenaline surged, and he was wide awake. He caught the sound of a distant howl on one side, then a closer one on the other.

"Hyenas!" hissed Tita. Dismayed, Mu saw that the wounds from the ants had bled again since he had washed at the spring.

"What can we do?" whispered Mu, his stomach knotting up with the same fear he felt when running from the policemen at the hospital.

"There are at least six, too many for Botu to fight off alone. But hyenas are cowards. They will come forward slowly, and won't attack until they are sure of the battle going their way. That may give us time."

"Time for what?"

"Time for reinforcements."

Now Botu was up. Suddenly he burst into a fit of fierce barking on one side of the anthill. Then he quickly ran to the other and barked in that direction. Then south and then north. He seemed to be either sending a message for help, or trying to create the impression that there were four dogs rather than one. By now Mu could see the sloped backs of two large hyenas as they scuttled behind a clump of brush some thirty meters away. One turned its head and its eyes, cruel and small, caught the moonlight. Botu continued to bark, growl, and otherwise sound as fierce as possible. Mu crawled to the top of the anthill, and from that vantage he could see three more hyenas approaching the same clump, and another two trotting in from the west.

"I count seven," whispered Mu. He scrambled back down the anthill and filled his pockets with rocks. "I wish I had brought my slingshot," he thought, remembering the long hours he had spent watching his great-uncle's goats. In those days nothing fiercer than a stray dog had appeared, but he used to pass the time using a certain leaf or rock for target practice.

Now the hyenas had formed a group, and the first two

began to advance, howling and sniffing. As they crept forward slowly, Botu suddenly charged at them from the mound barking angrily. The hyenas retreated a few steps and Botu withdrew. A minute later four hyenas returned, advancing steadily toward the stalwart Botu. When they came close enough, Mu began to throw his rocks. The first only grazed the flank of the leader, but the second hit another hyena squarely between the eyes. It let out a surprised yelp, and Botu seized the moment of distraction to spring on the leader.

Botu and the hyena rolled in the moonlight, panting and biting, but Botu had chosen his attack well and his jaws soon were crushing the windpipe of the hyena. Seeing their leader thus attacked, the others slunk back, but Mu knew the reprieve would be short lived. Within a minute the remaining six were advancing again, and this time the rocks that Mu flung did nothing to deter them. Botu released his grip on the now dead hyena, and backed protectively toward the anthill, growling.

Mu felt a curious disappointment that this should be the end of his story. Not fear so much as the sense of being cheated out of the many answers he knew Tita still had to his unasked questions about the amazing events that had befallen him, and the now ruined quest.

And that would have been the end of it all, except at that very moment something large and powerful and silent sprang from behind the anthill.

CHAPTER 9

Battle at the Anthill

In the bright moonlight Mu now watched a battle such as few humans have ever witnessed. Three lionesses had heard Botu's barks, and stealthily crept toward the hill. Perhaps Botu knew, or perhaps not, Mu was never sure. But just as the hyenas reached within striking distance, the lionesses sprang in one furious offensive. The night was suddenly rent with the howling of the hyenas, the snarling of the lionesses, and the barking and growling of Botu. For a few moments the spotted gray bodies of the hyenas mingled with the tawny lean forms of the lionesses and Botu's light yellow fur. Dust puffed up, grunts, scuffles, yelps. Another hyena lay motionless before the remaining five retreated. They paused at the clump of brush where they had originally grouped, watching the lionesses.

Then it occurred to Mu that he was perhaps no safer than he had been before—the lionesses were hunting together, and very likely they drove the hyenas off so they could feast on him instead!

Just as this thought was forming he heard Tita chuckle. "Impeccable timing, my friends, even I was beginning to fear that we would not survive this encounter. Greetings, greetings, *mulimutya, abheka bhaliyo*?" he concluded, the recent terror now giving way to his usual good manners.

One lioness turned to answer while the other two crouched carefully eyeing the waiting hyenas.

"We are well, the pride is thriving. With five cubs to feed we are kept busy most nights," she laughed, "but never too busy to answer the calls of a friend." Mu actually only heard gutteral grunts and growls, but Tita thoughtfully translated into his ear. "These hyenas will not

67

be easily dissuaded from following you, I'm afraid. They do not mourn their dead, but they do hate to miss the opportunity of a kill. They are puzzled now at our hesitation and will soon be back. Let us chase them east while you continue, and pray that we meet again. By dawn we should be able to reach you at the den."

"We are eternally most grateful for your timely assistance. May you be granted success in all your endeavors this night," bowed Tita. Then turning to Mu and Botu: "No time to lose. Tugende. Let's be off."

In the few remaining hours before dawn nothing else hampered their progress. Once when the branches of a tree rustled as they passed, Mu jumped and wondered what animal had marked their progress. But Botu trotted resolutely ahead and it was all Mu could do to concentrate on following. The moon was still well above the western ridge of hills when doves and kingfishers began to call out to the rising sun. A bright yellow weaver bird flitted across their path with a long blade of elephant grass trailing from his beak, already up and working on his nest-building.

"Tita, why do the hyenas attack and not the lions? The warthog listens to you, but not the mpali. I do not understand." Mu had been puzzling over these events for the last sleepy hour. In Mu's limited village experience, wild animals were wild, to be respected, but not to be expected to cooperate with each other or with humans.

"Yes, animals are animals for the most part and in most places. But it was not always so, and in the remotest plains of the earth there are still animals that are born to good or to evil. They do not choose one or the other as humans do, but rather certain lineages have been corrupted while others have maintained the peaceful coexistence that used to prevail in all places. On this savannah the hyenas are descended from a breed long ago bent by evil. And the lions are descended from a family that once walked harmoniously with an ancient race. In an hour of need, Botu knows the words to awaken the inherited memory of that pact, and you saw the results of that tonight. As a human boy you do not know which animals are which, so I advise you to treat all with caution and respect and distance. In fact, in spite of the gracious invitation of our friends, we will bypass their den. Botu and I are not sure of a certain male that moved in from lands south, where humans had hunted his kind. His animal instinct to preserve his den may lead him to act in such haste that we will not have time to explain our quest."

"And speaking of explaining our quest . . ." began Mu.

"All in good time, my boy, all in good time," murmured Tita.

Color now emerged from the shades of gray around them. Another brilliant yellow weaver bird darted past, and then Mu glimpsed a crimson splash among the blades of grass that turned out to be a red bishop bird. Lone cacti shifted palette from gray to dusty green, arms supplicating upwards. Mu's eyes felt very, very heavy. The dirt of the path and the spectrum of browns in the grasses began to blur . . .

"Mu!! Wake up!" Tita's voice sounded unusually urgent, and Mu became aware that he was stumbling. "Botu, Botu my friend, we must hold counsel," called Tita.

Mu stopped, and Botu turned back. "The boy is tired. And it is dangerous for all of us to bring him through this country at a stumble. His reactions are sluggish. He's had little food and no sleep."

Botu yelped and panted something that Tita seemed to understand.

"We will wait here. The river is near and Botu knows a certain elephant family. He has suggested a solution that should suit us well indeed."

"Elephants!" exclaimed Mu. "I thought you said we would see them from afar and avoid them. I thought they were dangerous. I know that the people in our villages used to hunt the forest elephants in our great-grandfather's time."

"Yes, but remember Botu knows the ancient and universal language, and if he finds this group reasonable he can ask for help. There is a strong maternal instinct in the elephant that which can make them very dangerous if their young ones are threatened. But if Botu can persuade them that you should be mothered and protected, well then, we have all that power and paranoia on *our* side. You see, danger can be a relative term."

It was not long before Mu heard a swishing crunch and became aware of branches swaying in a clump of bush some forty meters away, a phenomenon that could not be attributed to the faint breeze. Then the branches disappeared, torn off by the muscular supple trunk of a large elephant. She stepped into the clearing, flapping her ears against the ever-present flies that were reviving their activity in the growing warmth of the early morning light. Almost under her heels a medium and then a very small-sized version of herself appeared. Then from another bush to the left came two more large tusked beasts, and three more miniatures.

"Ah, I see congratulations are in order, Njogu has produced this year as has her sister. Their group now numbers three adults and five calves; a good size group for us, small enough to mobilize but large enough to intimidate. Just right."

The eight elephants now came forward across the clearing. The bulkiness of the adults made them appear to move in slow motion, while the calves combined forward trots with sideward play, rubbing heads, and tossing dust onto their backs with their trunks. They managed to appear completely at ease, moving with grace and confidence, but Mu knew they were also sniffing the air and monitoring for any threat. Botu trotted respectfully at the rear of the group, tail up and looking somehow very pleased.

After what seemed to be a formal greeting and parley with Tita, it was agreed that Njogu would carry Mu on her back as far as the forest edge, which they estimated would take most of the day. Botu, who could move more quickly without responsibility for Mu, would scout ahead and find a resting place. Mu supposed that Botu must rest sometime too, his wounds from the night before were slight but the exertion of the battle and travel must surely catch up with any living creature. The main sticking point of the negotiation seemed to be the method by which Mu would ascend to Njogu's back, since she categorically refused to kneel in the presence of such an unworthy creature as himself. Tita finally determined that Mu could climb a tree to reach the proper height. That is how Mu found himself spread out on the tough, gray, and very dusty hide of an elephant nearly four meters above the African plain, headed into the unknown.

CHAPTER 10

An Elephant's View

At first Mu could do little but worry about staying aloft. Njogu swayed as she walked, and the planting of each powerful, heavy foot sent shock waves through her body that rattled Mu's bones. But he soon realized that her back was very broad, and a slight shifting to one side or the other did not bring him within danger of falling. He leaned forward, nearly onto her head, and once when he shifted a bit more than usual her ear flapped back as if to catch him and her trunk was raised quickly to steady him. In this way his confidence grew.

From this height the savannah took on a new character. He could see grassland stretching into the distance, seemingly forever to the north and behind them to the east. To the south the plain was broken by the darker colors of the riverside vegetation, and he saw that their westward path paralleled the river and directed them toward the distant ridge of the mountains. As the sun rose higher, the grasses took on a waving golden hue. Mu laughed, at first startled and then delighted as springy oribi vaulted above the grass, darting away from the path of the elephants. The small antelopes seemed to combine a healthy sense of "we're so small we must run from every noise" and "we're so small you needn't bother with us so let us stare at you now that we're at a safe distance." The larger hartebeests with their twisted horns and long mournful faces also avoided the elephants, glancing up from their grazing in wonder at the strange creature on Njogu's back and then going back to their meal.

Soon the rhythm of Njogu's stride lulled the exhausted boy. He had drunk most of the rest of his water and eaten the fruit and honey gathered the evening before. Mu slowly leaned further and further forward, until he was sprawled on Njogu's neck fast asleep. As sleep overcame him the basket dropped from his hands and was deftly swooped up by the adolescent daughter of Njogu. Thus the group strolled along for several hours, pausing to strip branches from acacia trees, constantly munching the leaves and bark as they moved along, while Mu was rocked into the deep sleep of exhaustion and rolling motion.

He was awakened abruptly by a spray of tepid water and the spluttering hiss of Tita.

"Really, Njogu, I must protest, this is no way to wake a guest!" Tita sounded indignant. Mu laughed to find himself still on Njogu who was standing in the shallows of the river.

She lowered her trunk again, then lifted it and sprayed water over her back. Mu realized she had stopped where overhanging trees would enable him to descend, so he quickly grabbed the branches and climbed down. The young elephants were rolling in the mud of the river's bank and then venturing into the water, retreating, spraying, teasing. The adults drank and cooled themselves, and Mu noticed it was just past the sun's noon zenith. He too refreshed his hot body in the river, though the water was not very cool. He removed his now very dirty, worn clothes, washed them out and put them back on wet. Tita showed him where to find a side pool where the water had seeped through a purifying filter of sand, so that he could drink and refill the bottles he found in the basket.

As he looked up from filling the bottles, he saw that Tita was talking to a type of bird he had never before seen. Its body was perhaps twice the size of a large rooster from home, but suspended more than half a meter above the ground on spindly black legs. Bright red stripes decorated the long black bill, and even as it listened to Tita it stepped onto a shallow sandbar, stretched its wings, and grasped a snail from the riverbed.

"This saddle-billed stork has lost its mate, so her eggs are unfertilized. She is willing to give them to you to eat. We will follow her."

They were led to a basket-like nest of dried grasses arranged in the fork of a riverside tree, where three large eggs rested. Mu carefully lowered them into his basket, and bowed in gratitude. The stork returned the bow, this time with striking black and white wings spread to their full width. In the blazing noon sun, Mu found a hot, flat rock and cracked one egg onto it where it lay sizzling. Within a few minutes the egg was cooked, and he sprinkled it with a pinch of salt from one of the packets the cook had wrapped. Gingerly lifting the fried egg with a green stick, he could barely wait until it cooled enough to handle with his fingers before devouring it. He was so hungry he decided to cook the second egg right away too, but resisted eating the third as he found himself thinking gratefully of Botu's bravery during the night, facing the hyenas. It was the first time he could really offer the dog anything, and he looked forward to bringing him the egg.

All this time the elephants were bathing and drinking, resting and playing. Now less hungry, Mu could enjoy their antics. The mothers were ever watchful, but the smallest two seemed oblivious to anything besides each other and the fun of the mud.

"Tita, where are we going?" asked Mu. The adventure since leaving the hospital compound had offered little opportunity for questions. Now fed and clean and not sensing immediate danger, Mu dared to think a bit ahead.

"Toward the mountains, my son; your quest lies toward the mountains."

"Are we still being pursued?" asked Mu, remembering the men in police uniforms.

"Oh, yes, Abaddon will not give up easily. But it will take time for our enemies to realize you have gone into the savannah, even if spies have already betrayed us. Did you notice the vervet monkeys who scurried from the trees we passed before dawn? But our trail will not be easy to follow since you are leaving no prints or scent when you ride on Njogu. So do not fear."

Again Mu felt strangely comforted by those words.

"Tita, forgive my questioning, but I do not see how I could possibly have enemies interested in my whereabouts. The mukumu surely does not bother now that he received his payment, and he may not even know what happened to me. And the men who wanted me for some sort of work, well, they are dead. I thought maybe the police had been sent by their relatives because they believed I brought a curse that caused the accident, but if I disappeared into a land of wild animals surely they would be satisfied that they had been avenged. I cannot imagine who would be looking for me."

"That is because you cannot imagine who you truly are."

Tita did not continue, but left that intriguing statement hanging in the air, perhaps amused by the rising curiosity of his young charge. Mu waited, sensing that sometimes silence would bring more information than direct questions. But Tita remained silent.

"Who am I, then?" he finally burst out.

"Mu, my child, I have given you more facts about that in the last few weeks than you ever had before. Knowing the names of your parents is a start. But as to who YOU really are, well, that is not a question easily answered for any human. Your people have lost their orientation, and no creature can restore it for you. You must find that out for yourself."

This conversation gave Mu plenty to ponder as he climbed back onto the elephant and the group set off again across the plain. The evaporating water from his wet clothes cooled him for a while. He tried to ration his water carefully, but the relentless sun soon parched him. In the late afternoon, though the sun fell to a more bearable angle, the stored heat of the day radiated from the ground. Mu felt slightly dizzy, the rough hide of Njogu creasing as her ears flapped, the crunching sound of the elephants grazing as they went, the soft rustle of wind in the grass . . .

Suddenly Njogu stopped abruptly, trumpeted a terrible scream, threw up her trunk, and pawed the ground with her massive forefoot. The other two adult elephants immediately trumpeted and closed ranks while the calves ran back toward safety. Directly in front of them a massive Cape buffalo rose from his nap in the grass, and he was NOT happy.

CHAPTER 11

A Crater and a Cave

The buffalo eyed them, then lowering his head, pawed the ground. Mu remembered that Tita had listed the Cape buffalo as among the most dangerous of the plains animals, particularly solitary males who wandered separately from the herd. Njogu again trumpeted a scream, and for a moment there was a stalemate as they both stood their ground. But Njogu had her progeny to protect, and she was not going to be deterred. Rider or not, she charged forward.

Now Mu screamed, terror stricken at the sudden speed and seeing the short distance between him and the deadly buffalo close rapidly. Just when he thought he was going to either bounce off and break his neck, or be trampled by the buffalo, the beast turned and trotted away. Satisfied, Njogu came to a halt, shaking her ears and snorting angrily in the buffalo's direction until he was out of sight.

Even Tita seemed rattled. "Remember, my boy, a dangerous animal is a great asset when she is on your side," he lectured, trying to regain his customary calm demeanor.

"I don't think I would like to see that again," confessed Mu. "The noise alone was enough to scare *me* almost to death."

Njogu, however, appeared completely recovered as she returned to her family. The small ones were skittish for the next half hour; their mother's reactions had unsettled them. But nothing else of importance crossed their path for the rest of the afternoon. It was late in the day when Mu found he could make out a darker line on the horizon, though the setting sun made it difficult to see clearly. He shielded his eyes and decided that this was the forest of which Tita had spoken, though there also seemed to be hills in the near distance. And once again he found himself eager to see Botu, and was aware of how much he had missed the dog all day.

Now Tita seemed to be giving directions to Njogu. The elephants veered slightly north, away from the river. As Mu looked behind he realized that the ground had sloped upwards all day. Ahead, hills became more distinct, green mounds of grass with broad tops. Now the elephants moved more slowly, and Mu sensed they did not prefer this terrain and were eager to be done with their transporting duties. When the rise in the ground became steeper Njogu again stopped by an acacia tree, and Mu realized it was time to dismount.

"Tita, this is an acacia, full of thorns!" exclaimed Mu. "How can I climb here? Is there no other tree?"

"I see your point, my boy. For me, I just walk around those spiky thorns, but for you it will be challenging. Let me think . . . yes, the vines, some of these trees have liana vines that you could use to swing down. Njogu, let's try that one over there," he began and then switched to a language Mu could not understand. But Njogu could, because she patiently sauntered over to another tree; this one covered by thick vines. As she stood waiting, Mu tested them against his weight and found one that seemed secure. Holding it like a rope he was able to shimmy down to the safety of the ground. Immediately the savannah felt thicker, more closed in, and he realized what a privilege he had had to move through the grasslands at elephant height all day.

Mu bowed and murmured such thanks as he could imagine would be appropriate to a queenly elephant like Njogu. Evidently Tita translated, for Njogu flapped her ears in a friendly but final manner and turned to go, followed by her retinue. Now Mu found himself feeling very vulnerable and alone without even Botu.

"Upward we go. Head for the crater, you can follow that kob path," instructed Tita.

"Crater? What do you mean?" Mu began to walk up the slope, following an indistinct trail in the short grass. There were smatterings of trees now on the hillside, and the grass seemed to be cropped to ankle height. Some scorch marks on the tree trunks led him to guess that fire had passed this way in the last month or so, and the short brilliant green grass was fresh growth.

"These hills are not yet the true mountains, but on this side of the range there were once volcanoes. Many of these hills have a crater at the top where the volcano erupted and collapsed."

"Are we in danger, then?" Suddenly the burned marks seemed ominous, no longer a typical cyclical fire started by lightning strikes but evidence of deadly lava flow.

Tita chuckled, as only a chameleon can chuckle in one's ear, a very reassuring sound. "No, no, these volcanoes have been dormant for many, many generations in the lives of men; no, there is no danger of eruption. Of course, we are always in danger in this world, but at this particular moment you needn't worry about volcanoes. Just walk!" Tita seemed eager to make progress. Now that they were on the face of a hill, they found the shadows lengthening quickly as the sun fell behind the ridge of the crater above. Mu's meal of two eggs seemed long ago, and he had to force himself to keep walking as the path steepened. He was thirsty now too, but the bottles were empty. There were no signs of springs or streams and he remembered that the river was now some distance away. The bright green of the new grass faded with the daylight, so that by the time they reached the rim, the trees were merging into gray.

Below, in the crater, they saw a lake, still glimmering orange from the setting sun. It was a welcome sight indeed to a thirsty boy and his anxious companion. The kob whose path they had followed were bunched just below the inside of the crater's rim. Evidently having already drunk, they were settling down for the night in the longer grass, hoping to be protected from unfriendly eyes. Mu thought he could make out the stripes of a dozen or so zebra by the water's edge, some drinking, some playing games of charge and butting heads. He laughed, partly at their antics, partly at the relief of seeing water. He began to pick his way down the steep slope.

They reached the water's edge just as the first stars were emerging to reflect in the lake's surface. The waning moon would not rise for another hour, so Mu settled down to fill his bottles, drink, and rest in the dark gap between daylight and moonlight. He splashed his face with the water but this time did not want to get fully wet. Already the night felt cool and he worried about his scant clothing and lack of a blanket as their path climbed into the hills. He was leaning against a log watching zebra stripes meld into a uniform gray and then disappear when he heard a familiar bark.

"Botu!" Mu turned to look for the dog.

"I was beginning to worry that we had chosen the wrong crater," Tita confessed as Botu stood before them. He was clearly relieved. The chameleon and the dog had their own conversation; Mu guessed that they were catching each other up on the details of the day that had elapsed. Finally Tita switched back to Mu's language.

"Botu reached the craters some hours ago. He's scouted the area and reports that the baboon colony that used to exist in the cliffs and caves of the next crater is now deserted, for unclear reasons. He did find there a few human artifacts, a coppery button and a spoon. So perhaps hunters or smugglers drove the baboons from their caves. Whatever the reason, the shelter is a good one and we will take our next rest there. Fill the bottles because the next crater, the one with the cliffs and caves, is dry. Beyond that there will not be water again until we are in the true forest."

Mu remembered his gift, though he found himself shy again in front of Botu, his old fear returning. He tentatively held out the egg, and was relieved when Botu wagged his tail appreciatively and ate it in two bites, shell and all. After filling the water bottles and drinking as much as possible, they moved out, Botu leading the way on a path that spiraled back up to the crater's rim.

At the crest they could see the moon rising. A rippling white path appeared across the crater lake and seemed to tempt them to return east. But Botu turned down the outside of the rim. In the starlight Mu had to test every footstep, bracing his feet against the dewy cool tussocks of grass. They dipped down to the bottom of a saddle between the two old volcanoes, then began to climb again to the second crater. Just as Botu had explained, this one did not contain any signs of water, the bottom was deep in shadow and very quiet. Not even frogs could be heard in the still air. Again they found what seemed to be a path, a bit stony but nearly bare of grass, around the rim of the crater. This one was larger than the first and Mu guessed that it would take several hours to walk all the way around it. But before they had gone even a quarter of the way they took a branch of the path down the inside slope and found themselves facing a wall of rock.

The moon was high enough now, and at a good angle from the east to illuminate an impressive face of rippling cliff. Shadowed crevices, jagged ledges, some sheer drops, other faces broken by the clutch of a tenacious tree or two, the cliffs stretched as far as Mu could see in the moonlight. Botu led them along a ledge and then his white fur disappeared into the shadows.

Mu inched cautiously along, feeling the rock wall with his hand. Just where Botu had seemed to disappear he found that a cave opened in the cliff wall. Inside, the air was warmer; the rock retained the day's heat and the interior was sheltered from the night breeze. Botu had evidently gathered some food for them, and Tita even allowed a fire in this deserted, protected cleft. Carefully placing the brushwood that Botu had gathered, Mu used his old goatherding skills to start a fire from sparks. Soon they were warming their hands and then roasting the guinea fowl Botu had stashed for them there. Mu had plucked many a chicken in preparing dinner for his great-uncle, but the guinea fowl's feathers were nearly impossible to remove. He did his best, however, tucking the most impressive polka-dotted feathers into the buttonholes of his quickly deteriorating (formerly pink) school shirt. The rest of the quills he hoped would burn off in the roasting process; which they did.

Mu later remembered that night as one of the happiest of his life. A full stomach, a glowing fire, the security of the cave, Tita's stories, and the added warmth of Botu as they lay together to sleep—he dared to hope they might just stay there forever.

But that was not to be.

CHAPTER 12

Into the Mountain Forest

As the sun rose and awakened at least a dozen different species of birds, they seemed to compete with one another to be the loudest in announcing the new day. Mu sat up sleepily and Botu stretched his legs then stood to arch and stretch his back, tail wagging slowly as he shook off the night's sleep. Mu remembered his wish to stay in the cave, which had seemed so cozy the night before. He was about to suggest this, when Tita began his morning pep talk in his most schoolmasterly tones. Time to get on with the quest, etc. Mu sighed. He had no particular vision for where they were heading, other than the maddening hint that he did not know who he was. The fear of what they had left lessened as the daylight increased. He ate the avocados Botu had procured the day before, and stoked the fire to roast some starchy roots that reminded him of cassava. By the time they had thrown the avocado pits down the cliff and stamped out the fire, the sun was warm and the birds had settled into a more subdued daytime volume.

That day they climbed back out of the crater. There was no sign of the baboons, nor of any other animal. After skirting the rim again for an hour, they turned westward; a temporary descent from the lip of the crater led them across a saddle ridge. The grass was short here, but Mu picked his way with care where bright pink flowers obscured a painfully sharp thorny shrub. Soon they began a steady climb. Before the sun could become too oppressive, their path entered the shelter of trees. Mu realized they had reached the dark line of the forest's edge he had seen from Njogu's back the previous evening.

Once in the forest the path began to climb in earnest. Mu found himself having to grasp tree roots with both hands to pull himself up the steep slope. The trees were mahogany along with other species he did not recognize, but they were uniformly ancient, massive, and imperturbable. Their shade kept the undergrowth manageable, though one could not see very far in any direction. Where the occasional sunbeam streamed through, there were flowers—delicate pink or nodding purple orchids, and occasional sprays of white star-shaped blooms. Tita pointed out edible fruits and berries. Once they glimpsed the white-tasseled tails of colobus monkeys high in the canopy, but within moments the shaking branches and scramble of leaves quieted as the troop deftly disappeared. Every few minutes Mu had to stop to catch his breath; the steepness of the incline and the effect of the rising altitude combined to leave him gasping. A few times the forest opened to give spectacular views back east over the craters and the savannah beyond, and in these places Tita allowed longer breaks. Botu and Mu gratefully swallowed the water that Mu carried. His relief in a lightening burden, however, was balanced by his concern for replenishing the supply.

Before noon they reached their first spring, and though Tita advised a long drink and full bottles he also assured Mu that water was plentiful up in the mountains. While resting, Mu could marvel that he had looked at these very mountains, albeit the westward slopes, his entire life without once considering what it would be like to actually climb on them. He knew that a few hunters ventured up the lower slopes from villages near his great-uncle's, and returned with the coveted meat and fur of certain monkeys or mongooses. But for the most part the mountains had formed a steady backdrop to existence, seldom entering his conscious thought. Now he wondered how far the forest continued, and what kinds of birds or animals inhabited this place.

"How much farther will we climb?" he asked Tita, an impatient edge to his tone.

"Much farther," laughed Tita, which hardly seemed an encouraging answer.

True to prediction they began to pass frequent streams, some easily hopped over, others requiring wading and careful footing. Around noon they reached a ridge where the forest transitioned suddenly into a bright green cathedral of bamboo. Thin straight rods of bamboo, notched, a hundred hues from black-green to yellow-green, rose all around them.

J. A. Myhre

Fringy leaves made a hypnotizing pattern as they shimmered in the sunlight. This part of the forest was brighter than the slopes they had climbed all morning, and the path leveled as they followed the ridge.

The rest of the afternoon they continued in the bamboo. Botu ran ahead and doubled back periodically, apparently checking for the proper path. They drank frequently when meeting streams, and ate from the roots and fruits they found in the forest, but Mu was beginning to feel distinctly hungry for something more substantial. As the sun slanted lower through the bamboo, Mu felt an unfamiliar chill in the air. He had never been at this altitude, and wondered just how cold the night would become.

Before evening Botu led them to a cleft in the mountainside where a stream rushed down. From the stream, bare rock rose up in a sheer face, but near the bottom there was a cave-like shelter where the rock sloped out and overhung a dry dirt area. Here they built a fire. Botu disappeared as he had the night before, and this time returned with a rabbit. It was no small feat to skin the rabbit with a sharp rock, but once roasted and sprinkled with salt the meat was satisfyingly delicious.

The darkness gathered quickly as the fire burned low, and Mu was grateful to once again snuggle into Botu's warm fur for the night. Without the dog he doubted he would sleep at all at these cool heights. He had only slept what seemed to him a short while when a commotion woke him. Botu moved, barked, scuffled; Mu jumped up, disoriented. Then his mouth went dry and his heart dropped as he perceived the outline of a hooded black cobra in the moonlight.

CHAPTER 13

A Cobra, a Bog, and a Cage

The forest cobra was nearly invisible under the cave-like ledge, and the embers of the fire had died down to gray ash. But the moon had now risen, and Mu could see the lean dark body of the snake, writhing slowly, head up, hooding its neck to appear even more intimidating. Botu barked again, then growled, and stiffened in readiness, which broke the spell of fear that had paralyzed Mu. He picked up a partially burned branch from the edge of the fire and raised it over his head. Most snakes, even cobras, would have slithered off at lightning speed into the rocks by now. Most would not have approached the fire, though Mu had on occasion seen the swollen limbs of children bitten at night by snakes at home. Those types were certainly less venomous than the forest cobra: they easily entered the mud and wattle huts of the village looking for warmth and then sank their fangs defensively into the thrashing limbs of sleepers on their mats on the floor. This knowledge flashed through Mu's mind in an instant: this snake had perhaps approached for warmth when the fire had nearly disappeared, and now it must have felt cornered, trapped, and therefore extremely dangerous.

Mu found that his palms were sweating profusely in spite of his mouth feeling parched. He and the snake held their poses for another moment, neither backing down nor striking first. Then the cobra's head shot forward, and before Mu could react Botu pounced. There was barking, dust and ash scattered up;

Botu lunged forward and retreated again, forward and retreated, again and again. Mu caught glimpses of the black rope of the snake in the moonlight.

Within seconds it was over, though afterwards Mu recalled that the battle seemed to take an hour. Botu stood calmly erect, panting a bit, alert, unharmed. And the snake lay twisted on the ground, a few convulsive twitches running through its dead body.

Mu lowered his branch, now trembling at the nearness of death. He reached out to stroke Botu's head shyly, and thankfully. He was still not sure about this fierce friend, but it was hard to argue against the actions of the dog to save his life three times (from the police, the hyenas, and the snake), possibly four if the crash was included. Botu seemed to understand this growing tenderness, and wagged his tail in Mu's direction. Then he lifted the inert body of the snake in his mouth, trotted a few meters from the camp, and tossed it as far as he could into the bushes. While Botu was disposing of the snake, Tita at last managed to utter a few words.

"It's a bit difficult for me to move well at night in these temperatures, my boy, so if that snake was thinking of me for a snack there's not much I could have done to avoid it." Tita was matter-of-fact about the danger.

Mu remembered what he had been told about animals in general. "Was that snake just a snake, or something more?" he wondered aloud.

"I'm afraid that I must conclude there is more evil afoot here than the natural animosity between snakes and humans. The cobra behaved as if it were trapped, but physically it was not, it could have run from us. Something was compelling it to attack . . ." Tita ended in muttering. "Well, if there's any possibility of sleeping, we should at least try."

Before settling down again, Mu decided to stoke the fire back to life. He felt safer with the light as well as the warning heat, and hoped it would discourage any further visits that night. Then he laid down beside Botu once again, more grateful than ever for the warmth of Botu's body, the cushion of his side, and the alertness of his senses. He lay awake for a long time, watching the moonlight make faint shadows outside the cave, listening to the irregular pops of wood burning in the fire, feeling the steady rise and fall of Botu's breathing. Though he was convinced that his racing heart would keep him awake for hours, the exhaustion of the climb soon overcame his vigilance, and he fell into a deep sleep.

The sun was already glowing pink on the eastern horizon when Mu finally shook off his recurring dream of a warm being next to him, a basket . . . and found that he was alone on the floor of the cave. Botu had gone to the stream to drink, and Tita was insisting that they walk a ways first before looking for food as a good way to warm up.

That day they once again followed ridges heading south and west, occasionally having to dip down into ravines crashing with abundant, exuberant waters. Mu glimpsed smoke of village fires in the early morning far below them. At first he had enjoyed splashing through the streams, but now with cold and fatigue he only wanted to find safe crossings on stones or logs.

"Are the rivers here always so, so FULL of water?" he asked Tita. In his own village the rains were seasonal, and as far as he could remember he had left near the beginning of dry season. It had rained only a few times during his stay at the hospital and not at all since he left there, so the power of the water surprised him.

"These waters are ever flowing down from the snow. Glaciers still rest high above us, and though they have shrunk in recent decades they are still massive. There is never a dry season here. You may not have stopped to think about it, but your villages rarely experience the droughts that other areas do. The snow sustains life on both sides of the peaks."

Mu had heard of snow and certainly seen the white caps that grew and receded on the rocky peaks visible from his own side of the mountains. The haze of dust in the dry season or the heavy clouds of the rainy season often obscured the peaks, but when they emerged they always bore snow.

"Will we touch this snow? I have heard that it bites!" asked Mu, excited by the prospect.

"Our path is leading us gradually higher, as it must, and yet I doubt your ability to cross the pass without more protection than those old clothes. But yes, eventually, we shall have to pass through some snow." Tita did not seem quite so overjoyed at the prospect. "Now that we are higher, you must keep me inside your shirt from late afternoon, through the night, until midmorning. I cannot generate heat like you can, you know."

Mu felt a bit ashamed that in his excitement he had not considered the difficulties that snow would impose on a cold-blooded friend.

94

He wanted to ask more about snow, but suddenly the landscape changed completely. They had been hiking through the
morning, passing through bamboo and back into dark forest
where cobwebs of moss hung from the trees. Now the forest
suddenly ended in a field-sized bog. There in the sun grew
improbable plants that were spiky, purple, green. The grass
had a fresh smell in the cool air.

"Ah, you're in for a bit of tussock-jumping. Just follow Botu."
Now Tita was warming up in the unobstructed sunlight, and
able to even chuckle. "Watch your step, we go down together!"
he warned.

Tussock-jumping turned out to be a bit more demand-
ing than it looked from watching Botu. Botu leapt from one
spongy mushroom-like grass tuft to the next, avoiding the
swampy mud barely visible beneath the abundant vegetation.
Distinguishing tussocks from gullies was only the first challenge (made easier by having a dog to follow); the jumps were
at times long and more than once Mu found himself knee deep
in mud instead of safely perched on a mound of grass.

From the bog they caught a view of higher slopes and peaks
that had been obscured on the steep, forested ridges. No snow
was yet visible, so Mu knew that they still had a distance to
go before reaching the pass that Tita had mentioned. It took
them almost the entire afternoon to cross the bog hop by
hop, and rejoin a faint path on the other side. At this point
for the first time Mu noted a crossroad, a path that was crossing theirs.

"Who makes paths this high?" he asked. But Botu had his
nose to the ground, agitated, trotting a hundred meters up

each path and back, and he and Tita seemed to be conversing about the proper path. Mu's question was ignored.

For the next half hour they walked in silence, more quickly, but Mu sensed a new cautiousness. They pressed on in the fast failing light, and just when Mu felt he MUST ask about rest and food, Botu snarled and jumped off the path. Directly ahead they saw the sleeping form of a massive warthog, twice the size of any they had seen on the savannah. And ominously, the warthog lay in a tangled mesh of sticks and vine. He was caged.

CHAPTER 14

A Courageous Choice

For more than five minutes they stood perfectly still, not daring to make a noise or move an inch. Botu had taken cover in the bush, but his protruding nose was working at a frantic pace to sense any explanation for this most unexpected sight. Mu was at first concerned about the danger of the warthog, should he awaken. It was only later that it occurred to him to consider the danger of what or whomever had *caged* the warthog.

Finally Botu stepped back onto the path and approached the cage, slowly, almost sadly. Tita began to explain, in tones even hushed for a chameleon:

"This is Amani, the missing father of the warthog family which gave us shelter. He seems to be alive and yet captured for some reason we do not understand. Before we showed ourselves we wanted to be sure that there are no guards, or eavesdroppers. Botu now thinks the coast is clear."

"But he is far, far from where we saw his family!" puzzled Mu. He supposed that even a very direct path and fast pace would still put at least two days between the den on the savannah and this cage.

"Yes, we knew that he had been missing for some time. Let us awaken him quietly and hear what has happened."

Botu proceeded to utter short barks and growls, near to Amani's ear. At once the warthog sprang to his feet, his powerful body poised on short legs, his tusks looking even more intimidating now that he was awake. When he saw his company, he visibly relaxed. A long conversation of sorts followed, though of course Mu could not make out any of the details. At last Tita gave him a condensed version: the warthog had heard news of poachers or bad men of some sort moving on the borders of the savannah. It seemed that Amani held some sort of leadership position among a council of animals that had been summoned, that part was not clear, but en route to the council he had been surrounded by a dozen armed men. They did not shoot him, but used sticks and knives to corner him and hobble his feet with a rope. Then he had seen that they had subdued two duikers and three kob in a similar manner, all bore marks of having been beaten. The menagerie was driven in this way, roped and beaten, for several days. One night the first duiker was killed, cooked, and eaten by the men, and the second night the other. Two of the kob were left in a cage like this one at a lower altitude, and the third kob had been consumed by the group last night at their camp. Amani gathered from their behavior and what he could make out of their talk that their group regularly raided within wildlife preserves then brought edible animals to preset points on the mountain where the animals served as meat to sustain various bands of rebels who passed that way.

Mu knew from his limited knowledge of geography that the southernmost portion of this mountain range spanned the border between his country and its neighbor, though on the northern end it jutted into his own country. And he knew from talk around the mukumu's fire that remnants of a rebel network, comprised of ruthless and dissatisfied men bent on gaining power, still were rumored to move through the mountain passes. Even before Tita's story, he had absorbed the assumption that rebels were implicated in his parents' death, though now it seemed that the so-called attack on his parents might have been a cover-up for his great-uncle's revenge. Though he had no memory of open warfare in the area, he recalled that every year or two there would be threats of incursion and the army of his country would put on a show of reinforcing the border area. Then the rumors would dissipate and life would return to normal. He had never really seen a rebel, and most kids his age had begun to wonder if the talk was all a threatening story used to force obedience, such as when his aunts threatened "come straight home from school, the rebels look for boys who wander."

"Now, Mu, our quest has taken an unexpected turn, but here you have an opportunity to be of some use. Consider well and make your choice. I will tell you that Amani is more than what he seems, and to have him eaten by rebels would be a great loss, not only to his family, but also to life on the savannah. He is wise, and very strong, but he does not have the strength to break this cage."

"If he can't break it, how could I!" Mu could not help blurting out, bewildered.

"No one said anything about you breaking a cage, my boy. Patience. Amani watched the men. Though the cage is constructed securely from bamboo, you will note there is a gate with an actual lock. The lock has a key, which they hide under a certain stone just over there, so that another group can have access to their dinner. Whether that group is coming soon, or not for several days, we cannot know. Here is your choice: you can free Amani, or we can leave him here. Before you assume that you are bold enough for this task, let me remind you: when these men find that their dinner is gone, and that the cage is intact, they will know that some creature with hands has managed the key and lock. So if they then come upon us on the path, your already precarious position will be that much worse. These are men who serve Abaddon, though they may think they are only serving themselves. They are not likely to treat you well. Take a moment to weigh the risks and consequences."

Mu was mystified by this speech. He had taken orders for his entire short life, and no one had ever before presented a course of action to him as a choice. He was being asked to do something that, of the present company, only he could manage. That feeling of being needed flattered him—yes, he had thrown stones at the hyenas and raised his stick in front of the cobra. Those encounters had awakened a kernel of courage in his soul that he had not known before, but it was still a mere kernel. He paused, thinking of soldiers he had seen passing his village. They were not bad men he supposed, but their weapons made everyone give them a wide berth and respect. What would it be like to encounter similar men who were hungry and angry, and worse still, angry at him?

Tita waited patiently, Botu thumped his tail and sat by the door of the cage, Amani leaned down on his front knees to pretend to nibble at the grass growing through the bars of bamboo.

It was Mu's first taste of a free choice with important consequences, and he chose to act.

"Show me the rock," he said quickly, before any more fearful thoughts could crowd his mind. Botu led him to a stone that they easily turned over. A few beetles scurried into the dirt and he picked up the shiny key and walked to the cage. He hesitated a moment, seeing again the powerful body of the warthog, then reminded himself that this beast was not the enemy. He unlocked the door, and Amani exited at a dignified pace, as if he was merely leaving his home. Mu carefully relocked the door and hid the key, though he doubted that would fool anyone.

The boy, the dog, and the warthog all headed quietly up the path a few paces before Tita whispered to him to stop.

"Amani must leave us here. It is a regret for all of us, because you could learn much from his wisdom. But it will be safer for him to take his own course back down through the forests, and he longs to return to his family where he is needed. Our path continues upward."

Amani bowed again, and Mu felt a catch in his throat to realize that this tough and grizzled creature was thanking him. Tita assured Mu that he had sent all the proper family greetings, and without further delay they parted. Within seconds the warthog's upright tail disappeared into the forest. At Tita's urging they continued their climb at a quickened pace. Night had nearly fallen, and they had the sense that these men would be close behind them by now looking for their meal.

But that assumption proved fatally flawed—the band of rebels was descending from on ahead, and not a quarter of an hour after leaving Amani they walked straight into the path of the oncoming enemy.

CHAPTER 15

Child Soldier

Afterwards Mu would replay the terrible encounter over and over in his mind, straining for details that would help him make sense of the disaster. They had been climbing quickly, still in the forest, darkness seeping down through the canopy. They feared being followed, so every few minutes Botu would retrace steps backward and sniff carefully. A slight breeze blew up the mountain that evening, allowing Botu continual reassurances that no men followed below. They had come to a rather strongly flowing stream, and while Mu bent down to drink, Botu had retreated for another check behind. The noise of the water and the dim light provided a deadly combination: Mu never even saw the men until the crack of a firing gun exploded from just across the stream in front of him. In one instant he sprang up from drinking, he heard Botu yelp, and just as the white fur of the dog disappeared into the dark forest, a rough hand knocked him to the damp ground.

Tita was concealed in his shirt because of the coolness of the hour, one small detail that Mu could be thankful for. But Botu disappeared completely. Two men tried to track him for some time but returned panting. Mu did not know whether to feel elation because the dog had escaped, or despair because the dog had abandoned him.

There were ten men in the unit. When they had satisfied themselves that Mu was alone except for the now-departed dog, they spent no time talking to him at all, but conferred quickly among themselves. His hands were tied behind his back with sisal, and he was forced to march back down the path toward the cage. The men moved quickly, single file, alert. If Mu slackened his pace the man behind him jutted the butt of his rifle into Mu's back. No one spoke. It was completely dark by the time they reached the empty cage. No moon yet rose, and only a smattering of stars blinked through the leaves of the forest.

It was when they saw the empty cage that they really became angry. In a matter of minutes they deduced that this troublesome boy had interfered and most likely eaten the meal their comrades had promised was left there for them. They locked Mu into the cage now, which gave him reason to wonder if he was being considered as replacement meat. The dialect of the rebels was close enough to Mu's that he could understand almost all of their conversation, a fact that shocked him. He never considered that members of any clan he knew could be among the rebels. That first evening with the rebels, he kept quiet and watchful, never speaking, to prolong the time they spoke freely assuming his ignorance. As he shivered in the cage in complete darkness he learned several important facts about the group.

First, it was clear that these men were part of a larger organization. He kept hearing jumbles of letters, but DFM surfaced most often. He thought he had probably heard those letters before, but he could not put words to them that made sense. English, French, Swahili, or some local dialect? Defense Force of the Motherland, Democratic Forum Movement, Democratique Forces Militaire?? In fact the name made no difference. These were not government soldiers. They were men deployed high in the mountains, and any agenda beyond warmth and food seemed inconsequential to their conversation that night. Second, he felt sure that three of the rebels were boys barely older than he, perhaps fourteen or fifteen. Third, he sensed that they were moving up and down, and back and forth along the mountain ridges, and had camped in this spot often.

Some of the group argued for killing the boy right away, others for leaving him safely locked in the cage to die of exposure or starvation. To Mu's relief no one seemed eager to eat him instead of pork. From scraps of conversations at the mukumu's, he had long ago gathered that though cannibalism was a taboo subject, it was whispered to still occur in rituals for power. So it was with a sense of relief that Mu finally heard the oldest man state that the boy would remain in the cage until the morning, when he would get a better look and decide if he was worth preserving for recruitment.

This man, whom Mu later learned to call Mbongbo, was clearly the leader. He directed the others in pitching camp, building a fire, cooking a bean stew. No one seemed to take much notice of Mu once the decision to camp was made, but just as the moon finally rose, Mbongbo brought him a cup of the stew and a blanket for the night. In spite of his resolve to escape these enemies at the first chance or die doing so, Mu found himself so cold and tired and hungry that his child's heart immediately grasped onto the flicker of attention from the leader. Seeds of doubt or ambivalence were planted in that gesture the very first night.

For the next fortnight Mu moved with this group. When they reached a more permanent camp, he was given khaki fatigues like those soldiers wear, along with a sweater and shoes. This was out of practicality more than kindness. The camp's elevation made even days cool, and he would not have long survived the nights in his old pink school shirt and shorts. Several times on excursions he saw dustings of snow, but he did not feel the excitement or joy over this beauty that he had anticipated. His entire being was now concentrated on obedience and survival. His cousins and school days became memories he fought to return to at night, and by contrast with his current situation, life at his uncle's compound now seemed reasonable.

His training in the village served him well, though. He once again carried water, gathered firewood, peeled matoke, picked stones out of rice, washed clothes. No one spoke to him much, but the more useful he made himself the more comfortable they became with his presence. Occasionally he would spill water or burn food or be too slow, and if Mbongbo

noticed, there would be an angry outburst to survive, perhaps a smack on his head, a caning on his back, or a withholding of the meal's meager leftovers, which Mu normally ate when cleaning the pans. These disciplines were administered thoughtlessly and randomly, so Mu soon learned to stay out of sight and mind as much as possible.

He rarely dared to take Tita out of his shirt now. The chameleon seemed older, slower at this height. Mu tried to time his water gathering for midday so that Tita could rest in the sunlight by a stream and revive with a few insects and drops of water. But insects were less abundant at this elevation, and one of the armed adolescents was always assigned to follow Mu and ensure his return. Mu cried most nights, bitter that Tita's counsel seemed to be withdrawn now that he needed it most. In the first day or two Tita tried to cheer the boy, saying that what the Enemy meant for evil could be turned to good, since he now had more appropriate clothes and even a source of food for surviving in the mountains. Tita advised cooperation and watchfulness, seeming assured that an opportunity for escape would arise.

But as the days turned to a week and then the week to two, Mu looked for escape less and less. Adaptation is a skill of childhood: by the end of the fortnight to Mu the idea of a quest seemed like a silly dream—the reality of daily hard work and the safety of being part of the group seemed all that mattered. He found himself working for any sign of approval from Mbongbo. He no longer grumbled over the work he was given as "girls' duty." He was glad to be needed. Slowly the others also became accustomed to his presence.

At the end of the fortnight two more men joined the group, bringing the total to twelve plus Mu. These men held counsel with Mbongbo the afternoon they appeared. Their dress and speech matched the rest of the men, and they deferred to Mbongbo, so Mu surmised they were subordinates in the same DFM group. The next day there was a change in the air: guns were cleaned, targets set up for practice. Mbongbo ordered one of the adolescent recruits to show Mu how to clean and carry a gun. A few days later he permitted Mu to shoot twice at an empty tin they often filled with rocks and swung from a string over a tree branch for practice. Mu did not hit the can either try, but an important line had been crossed. He had fired a gun, and felt the thrill of its power. He felt a little taller, more important, and he suddenly was motivated to prove himself to the group. Tita tried to talk to him the next day when they were relatively alone, but Mu dismissed his weak concerns. He wanted to be a man, not a boy on the run. Tita sighed, but Mu no longer cared what the chameleon thought, a shift in heart whose consequences he could not foresee.

CHAPTER 16

Betrayal

The fortnight stretched into a month. The two newer men
did not stay more than a few days; they had evidently brought
messages, salt, and ammunition (which allowed Mbongbo
to permit the very limited target practice) and then moved
on. In all this time Mu did occasionally wonder about Botu.
Once or twice he thought he might have seen a glimpse of
that creamy fur between some rocks or under a bush. But
inevitably, by the time he ran to look, there was no trace of a
living creature. He heard the men speak of a dog-like spirit
that they felt inhabited this place and wished them ill—some
even went so far as to take a shot at this spirit, and others
suggested moving camp. Tita spoke infrequently now, and

sometimes a whole day would go by in which Mu forgot to take him out for feeding. When he did speak, he tried to counter Mu's growing identification with the group, tried to interest him again in his vague quest, but Mu listened half-heartedly. He was a boy who had never really belonged, and Mbongbo's group seemed to take him in.

Mu noted that groups of two or three men would occasionally be sent off from the rest for one or two days, and when they returned there would be meat in the form of freshly killed colobus monkeys, or rarely even a few chickens or a basket of potatoes. He supposed the men stole the latter from outlying farms. Though the area they patrolled was nearly uninhabited, a day's march north could bring a hungry rebel to slopes where the nature preserve was encroached upon by expanding agriculture. And there was no lack of colobus monkeys in the forest, though Mu could not imagine being quick and accurate enough to shoot one. He had initially refused to eat this bush meat, but hunger and the gradual acceptance of his new reality eventually eroded his resistance. Now he was as glad as anyone to see a raiding party return.

The day that Mu's new world fell apart began with a sense of foreboding. The dry season was drawing to a close, and heavy clouds had been gathering for about a week. That morning Mu heard thunder for the first time in the mountains, and found the sound much more unnerving than he had in the village. When a raiding party returned midday, they spoke in hushed tones with Mbongbo, and Mbongbo gave the word for a march. Breaking up camp was not difficult—the men did not sleep in tents but only moved with small plastic tarps, bedrolls, some dried food, pans. Within an hour they were heading down a trail that already was beginning to seem familiar to Mu. Mbongbo acted pleased, as if there was something particularly good they all had to look forward to. Two of the younger members of the group surmised that some particularly large or tasty animal had been stashed in the cage, since the path they had taken headed in that direction.

By early afternoon, rain began to fall—no, not fall, pound. The rainy season in the mountains began with a serious downpour along with gusts of wind that knocked leaves to the ground. The first small bog they came to was already knee-deep in mud. Mu shook his head wondering what the bogs would be like after several months of rain. Everyone grumbled.

Mu guessed it was about four hours past noon when the leader of the marching line called an astonished halt at the strong bamboo cage where Amani had originally been stashed. All the men had been hoping for food; instead they were shocked to find a dog. Botu sat calmly inside the cage.

Though Mu marched near the end of the line, he ran to join the rest around the cage, staring. Most of the men took it as a sign of great luck that this spectral hound was real flesh and blood, and, what's more, powerless in their grip. They covered their hesitations and anxieties with laughter as they talked about the dog and the times they had glimpsed it on the perimeter of the camp or trailing behind their line. Everyone agreed that the dog had first started to appear the day they found the boy Mu. They turned to Mbongbo to see what he would do with this prisoner.

"Is this your dog, boy?" he asked gruffly.

"No, sir, I do not have any dog." Mu felt a pang of guilt as he spoke, but technically Botu did not *belong* to him or anyone else for all he knew.

"Boy, this dog did us a service, he brought you straight into our hands only a day after we lost our last servant in an unfortunate fight. But since then it has done nothing but haunt our trails; it has disturbed us for too long. Our hunters were finally able to capture it. Do you know why I ordered them to leave it alive in the cage?" The question was clearly rhetorical. No one answered, a few looked interested, most merely pretended to listen while actually watching the dog. Mu shuffled his feet in the leaves and looked at the ground. He could not look at Botu who sat proudly, alert, unmoved. "I have long desired that we could watch the death of this dog together, to show that no spirit animal is able to disturb the plans of Mbongbo." Here there was a slight increase in interest from the men, as if something of a sport was about to ensue.

"And since this is not your dog, boy, I have decided to let you prove yourself at last. You have learned to hold a gun, but until you kill a living creature you will be just a boy playing with a toy. Today I am offering you the chance to become a man. This is the very creature who betrayed you to us. Now you can pay it back, and be initiated into the DFM as well."

Mu's heart sank deeper and deeper, a wave of nausea rose in his throat. He was barely aware of one of the men removing the small pack he carried on his back, and another handing him a gun. Did Botu really lead him to these men? Was this the purpose of the so-called quest all along? In his surreal state he did not consider the logical inconsistency of their desire to shoot an ally.

"To be sporting we should let the dog loose, but I think even a caged dog will be challenge enough for this boy!" joked one of the younger rebels.

Now shame washed over Mu, compounding his doubt. Was he man enough to hold a gun? Was this dog really his friend? Was Botu not the one who had pushed him from the truck and started this whole chain of events? Had he not always been on his own, fending for himself in this world? And at last anger joined the doubt and shame. Anger that this dog had put him in this position, anger that the others thought of him as weak.

He took the gun.

Silence descended over the afternoon forest. Even the cicadas stopped, no bird made a sound. Only the incessant dripping of the leaves after the midday rain continued.

He raised the barrel and looked down the sight, as he had been taught. It was not a particularly new gun, an old rifle really, with a crude sighting mechanism and a worn wooden butt.

He squinted one eye shut as he lined up the gun barrel with Botu's face.

Botu did not move, did not cower, did not run around the cage.

Mu stood equally still, the gun aimed, poised, his heart beating wildly, his palms wet with anxious indecision.

And then he did it. He pulled the trigger.

In that indescribably horrible moment, he heard the gun scream in his ear, he saw the dog thrown into the bars at the back of the cage by the impact of the bullet, and he knew his life was over. He had just made the worst possible mistake.

CHAPTER 17

Redemption

What broke Mu's heart as he pulled the trigger was this: Botu looked directly at him. And in those eyes he read not fear, not hate, not disappointment . . . but love. Botu forgave the boy even as he was betraying the dog to the death. Botu understood the predicament, the emotions, the confusion in the boy's heart. Botu understood Mu's petty, mean, shameful, self-centered, cowardly decision. And Botu loved him anyway.

Time seemed suspended in that moment of his failure, and of Botu's glory. Then suddenly Mu was on the ground, curled on his side, crying. The men were laughing. Someone had opened the cage and was dragging the bloody, lifeless body of the dog out. Mbongbo seemed agitated more than amused;

he kicked Mu roughly and told him to get up. Somehow Mu managed to stand.

"You're crying like a baby, stand up and be a man," Mbongbo growled at him. No one else seemed to bother with him at all, their attention was on the body of the dog, touching it at first tentatively then more boldly, choosing to forget their former fear of a spirit and finding relief in the dead animal's helpless appearance.

So Mu stood up. And he was a bit closer to manhood. Not because he had killed, not because he had stopped crying. He knew at that moment he had reached the bottom. He had chosen acceptance from the group over courage, the attention of killers over the faithfulness of a friend. He had come to the moment of truth about himself, and the truth was not beautiful. But in the very act of committing the worst deed of his life, he also saw something deeper than that truth about his own soul. He saw forgiveness, forgiveness given freely when he least deserved it. That look from Botu penetrated his soul, deeper than truth, deeper than guilt. So he stood as an emerging man, determined to return to his quest and leave these men at the first opportunity.

CHAPTER 18

Toward the Summit

The rest of the evening was a blur to Mu's numb mind. Somehow he found himself doing his usual menial work. The relief of the men in seeing the dog dead was short lived, within half an hour they forgot they were ever in awe of this beast and instead grumbled about the lack of an edible animal. Mu was grateful that they did not try to eat the dog. Though it was evening, he felt the need for Tita's comfort at the end of this disastrous day. He carefully took the chameleon out of his shirt and held it gingerly in his hands, warming it by the dying embers of the fire. Tita began to stir. Mu perched the chameleon on his ear, smiling in spite of the heaviness of his heart as he felt the delicate pincers of the chameleon's feet attach to his skin.

"My child, my heart grieves for you," began Tita. This was a most unexpected beginning to what Mu anticipated would be a stern lecture.

"Tita, perhaps you could not see. I have, I have . . . I have killed Botu." The words stuck in his throat and dry heaves of sobs began to shake his shoulders in spite of his resolve.

"Yes, that is why I grieve for you. You made a very, very wrong choice, my child. But you have been given the grace to know the wrongness of your action. The truest thing about you is not that choice, but your sorrow for it, and your acceptance of Botu's love in spite of it." Tita spoke very slowly, and paused often. "I know you. I know your sorrow. And I know your resolve to leave this group. Our time may be short this evening, so let us not dwell on your deed, which is complete and cannot be changed. Let us move on to our plan. You will need three things: the wool hat you see that young man wearing, yes, the red one. And matches. And a bit of food. That is all. And you will need to trust me. Do not fear."

Mu remembered those words from their first meeting. Fear had been such a part of his life, but he felt he had now done the worst, so fear was no longer necessary.

"I am not afraid. I don't know why I need those three things, but I will trust you. How can I get the hat?"

"Do not try and steal it, though the man you see wearing it stole it, you would not be right to perpetuate his action. Simply ask for it."

"Ask for it? These men all hate me!"

"Ask."

121

Mu tucked Tita back under his shirt and walked over to one of the adolescent rebels. He was not sure how to begin, but after some greetings and awkward pauses he simply blurted out his request for the hat. The young man was used to a life of give and take, favors asked and favors owed. He considered that it would not be a bad thing to have the group's servant beholden to him. He could claim it back at any time anyway, so he took the hat off his head and tossed it to the boy. Mu put it on.

That night Mu found it very difficult to sleep. Mbongbo woke the group before dawn and ordered a hot porridge be cooked, a rare luxury. Mu was so busy with this task that he did not hear much of the reason for the early start. Remembering Tita's instructions, he made sure that some matches and portions of posho flour and beans, as well as one *sufferia*, went into the pack he would carry. The men lined up single file for their day's trek. A few joked about Mu's hat. He tried to hang back as far as possible in line, but as usual he was not permitted to be last. Mbongbo usually positioned himself near the front and put his second in command at the very rear.

They climbed hard that day, leaving the forest by midmorning and clearing the last bog just after noon. When they stopped to drink, Mu dared to take Tita from his shirt, and Tita instructed that he wished to be placed under the hat clinging again to Mu's ear. Now Mu could guess the importance of the hat: it not only concealed Tita, but kept him warm in a position where he could easily speak and be heard by the boy. On and on they climbed, through areas of shorter shrubs and fantastic plants that Mu had never before seen nor heard of. The path was difficult to see, and by evening it was mostly loose rock and stunted pines.

Mu was shocked when, before sunset, they reached some crude shelters. He had never considered that the rebels might have bases so obvious, with stone and wood huts, cooking areas, and even some provisions. But as the sun sank and the cold turned from uncomfortable to dangerous, Mu saw that men would not survive long at this altitude without the slight increment in warmth a roof and walls could bring. They built a fire right in the center of the hut; a gap had been left in the roofing to allow the escape of smoke. The mountain range, he had been taught, spanned nearly two hundred kilometers from southwest to northeast, and at the widest point was forty to fifty kilometers across. Men could move for years in this expanse without being seen, so they made no attempt to hide this camp. No villagers climbed to these heights. The mountains were considered sacred ground by surrounding tribes; people feared the thunderous storms that rolled down their slopes, and held the mysteriously white peaks in awe.

That night, sleeping on the plank floor of the hut as close to the others as he dared draw, Mu dreamed again his recurring dream of being tucked comfortably into a basket with something warm and soft. But for the first time, in this dream he saw the source of the warmth. It was a puppy, and when he saw the puppy's eyes he was sure it was Botu. But before he could touch the dog, the basket tipped and he rolled out.

"Get up, you lazy boy!" a gruff voice was saying, pulling the blanket away and giving him a prod with his foot. It was

Mbongbo, who seemed to push them to earlier and earlier departures every day. He was only waking Mu at first, ordering him to make tea from the provisions they had found in the hut. Mu knew that Mbongbo had been displeased, disappointed in his emotional reaction to killing the dog, and sensed that his days of usefulness to the rebels were numbered.

As others awakened and drank the scalding hot liquid, Mbongbo finally gave a rough outline of their plan. They were starting well before sunrise because the waning moon provided good light at that hour, and they had a long and dangerous march. This was the day they would cross the pass, the highest walkable point in the range. The rains had begun, which meant there would be a chance of snow on the pass. Most snow this high fell only at night though, and the signs were good for a clear day. A southward path from the pass would enable them to rendezvous with two other groups by the next day. Precise timing was critical because all three groups had been assigned to attack a civilian target (they would not be told what target until the morning of the attack). Mbongbo did not actually mention the rendezvous or the attack; this was information Mu had gleaned from the men's conversations over tea. He remembered the hat, matches, and small food provisions when gathering his pack.

Soon they were walking in their customary line. Again Mu tried to get in the rear and look for his chance of escape, but to no avail. He resigned himself that escape would be suicide at this temperature, this far from home. But almost as soon as they began walking, Tita began to talk to him, under the hat, directly in his ear.

"My child, today is the day. You have not understood everything about your quest so far, and I did not plan to reach this
point in this company. Nevertheless, we are approaching a
crucial moment. I have prayed for snow, yes for a blizzard. Do
not fear."

And Mu did not.

CHAPTER 19

Through the Pass and Under the Falls

That day Mu reached the top of the world, or so he felt. It was one of the highest points on the continent. The sun rose behind them, brilliant. Mu expected to be able to see the ocean perhaps, but the lower slopes of the mountains were already shrouded in the mists of the oncoming rains, and beyond the growing light shimmered a mirage of colors without distinct form. The pass formed a saddle between two peaks ahead of them, mostly bare rock, lichens, low shrubs. And thankfully (they all felt) no sign of snow.

Tita now coached him almost continuously, advising hand and footholds when the path was dangerously steep, encouraging his breathless attempts to keep to the rebels' pace. The day was becoming less bright, clouds now obscured the peaks between which they were passing. Soon the entire world was cut off, and all that mattered were the hundred meters of path visible ahead. Then in weariness Mu could look only as far as the back of the man in front of him.

Then the snow began. Mu awakened this time to the beauty of the flakes falling. The ground looked like a threshing floor with a dusting of posho flour. The temperature kept dropping, and the snow's pace picked up. Mu could hear the men ahead and behind calling out complaints about their bad luck, asking Mbongbo how much farther to the top of the pass. A few minutes later the light became even dimmer as snow fell heavily. The entire ground was white now, slick. Progress slowed as the men struggled to keep sure footing. When the wind picked up, it became more and more difficult to see anything at all.

"This is our blizzard, my boy, sent just for us!" Tita chuckled. How a chameleon, even one as odd as Tita, could be happy in blowing snow on a steep slope puzzled Mu. He was too cold to even think of replying, not that he wanted to risk talking out loud.

"Now you must listen, and listen well. When I tell you to step to the right, do it. And then continue to follow my directions. Some of these men will not make it over the pass. When you are missing on the other side, they will assume you have slipped or frozen to death. No one will see us leave the line. Get ready. NOW."

Mu obeyed as quickly as his sluggish muscles could respond. He turned blindly right into the swirling snow. For the next

127

half hour Tita gave directions every few seconds: step up here, grasp the ledge you'll feel there, move left, turn a few degrees right, etc. The hat's importance was now very clear: without Tita's internal positioning sense, they would have been lost completely. Mu walked blindly, nothing but white air and white ground in any direction, unable to see beyond the length of his arm. It felt like years, but probably no more than an hour later the ground sloped less steeply.

"We have reached the top of the pass!" congratulated Tita. "Don't worry about running into the others—those that do not perish in the blizzard are also reaching the pass, but about a half a kilometer south of us. Put your arm out now, feel just ahead, there will be two boulders. Between them is a very narrow passage. That is our road. We will pass through to a different descent than the rest."

Sure enough, when Mu stretched out both arms, within a few steps he reached stone that rose higher than his head. Feeling carefully, he found the crevice and slipped in. The passage was narrow but not long, and they emerged into more snow on the other side, on a slightly descending slope.

"Keep your right hand on the rock wall, we will move north a few paces, and then you will find the entrance to a cave where we will wait out this storm."

The cave provided a welcome break from the biting wind. In spite of his hat and the long sleeves of the sweater and fatigues he wore, Mu was achingly, deeply chilled, a cold beyond his previous imagining, a cold that sapped his will. His cheeks stung from the snow; the flakes that had started as gentle, delicate marvels had been driven by the wind and felt like sandpaper on his face.

He retrieved the matches from his pack, and a bundle of sticks that Mbongbo had tied onto his pack that morning, laughing that they would take their tea on the other side of the mountains. Soon he was melting snow and cooking. He worried about Tita, but as the sticks began to burn, some beetles crawled from the wood to escape the heat, a perfect dinner for a chameleon. When Mu had eaten he lay as close as he dared to the dying fire and tried to sleep.

It was the sunlight that awakened him, the sunlight and the quiet. The cave's entrance faced west, more evidence that they had actually come through the pass. The wind and snow had ceased, and in their place a perfect stillness reigned. Mu could not hear anything at all, no birds, not even dripping water. He stretched and peered out of the crack in the rock. Before him he could see another ridge of distant peaks, at least twenty kilometers away. But between his ridge and that second more westward one, there was a valley. Not just a slight depression in the mountain range of peaks, but a deep valley. Below the snow line he could see dark green trees and perhaps even a lake in the distance.

"Tita, Tita, are you awake? What valley is this? I never heard of anyone speak of a valley among the peaks!"

Tita moved slightly under the red cap. "You will not find this valley on any maps of the village people, or even in school books, though if you listen closely to old songs and legends you might get a hint of its existence. The entrance is only by that narrow passage we came through this morning, and one like it on the western slope. Only those guided here will find it. We are safe now."

"Are we going there?" Mu found himself inexplicably attracted to this strange land, stirred by the frame of bare snowy peaks around this bowl of forest and lake. He felt its beauty as an ache almost, a longing in his soul that he had not known he had.

"What is a quest without a destination?" laughed Tita.

"But why? Will we find anyone there?"

"All in good time, my child, let's make some effort to get lower by nightfall."

Mu gathered the pan and blanket into his backpack and they set off.

Going down proved much faster, though still physically challenging. A few times Mu slipped and skidded. By evening they were back among trees, mosses, ferns, and streams. As they approached a larger creek, Mu looked for a way to pass without getting his shoes wet. Just upstream he saw a waterfall, perhaps ten meters high, splashing down into a pool.

"You won't find a way across this one. You must go through. This is the boundary water. You will find it bracingly cold but purifying. Remove all your clothes to keep them dry, and put them in your pack, on your head. Put me in too, and whatever you do, don't drop us! Now listen carefully. Carry the pack and put it down on the other side, then wade back to the waterfall. You must pass under the waterfall and pick up the white stone you will find inside."

This enigmatic direction was all Mu could pry from Tita. Reluctantly, because of the cold, he removed the shoes and clothes he had received from the rebels, and packed Tita carefully in his bag. The stream proved to be about chest deep, and he picked his way carefully, holding his breath because of the chill of the water. When he reached the opposite bank, he leaned his pack against the tree without leaving the stream, and then waded up to the falls.

From below, the ten meters looked ten times higher. He put his hand out to feel the spray, and the power of the water frightened him. He could swim a little, but wondered how long he

would have to hold his breath to pass through the water. The deepest part of the pool at the bottom had been only slightly deeper than the point where he crossed, so he had not had to get his head wet yet. Mu stood for a long while, watching the drops of water suspended in the air and then crashing down to the pool. The light in the forest was golden, a hue that indicated he might have less than an hour of daylight left. His feet were already numb.

At last he summoned his courage and stepped into the crashing, deafening, pounding weight of water, suffocating, pushing him down . . . And then he was through. Behind the waterfall the damp rocks glistened black. He could not see the forest now through the thick curtain of water. The floor of the cave behind the waterfall sloped upward; here the water was only knee and then ankle deep. And there in the furthest reach of the cave, he saw in the dimness a white stone, incongruous among the dark rocks of the stream. He picked it up. It was smooth, and fit perfectly into his palm. Looking at it, he turned it over.

There was writing on the stone. Carved into the surface of the rock in ornate letters he read one word, a name: Mujuni. Mujuni, savior. Who could this be, or what? He had heard the name before, though it was not very common. Perhaps he was meant to take the stone to someone named Mujuni.

Then somehow, in his heart, he knew, this was *his* name, his true name. The name his parents whom he could not remember now had given him. Mujuni.

CHAPTER 20

Journey's End

Mujuni emerged from the waterfall, clutching the rock. The numbness had reached nearly to his knees, but somehow he managed to climb out on the far bank, shivering. Now the air was suffused with pink; he could hear birds coming home to roost, evening fell. Using the blanket to dry off as best he could, he put on every piece of clothing and shivered still to regain warmth. It was too late to descend much farther. At Tita's instruction he began collecting brush from the forest floor as they went along. That evening they slept in a tree. Not in the branches, but actually inside the massive trunk of a *mvuuli* tree. An old fire had burned a large hollow into the core, but the tree remained alive. Mujuni wondered a bit about what other animal might come in the night to claim this den, but Tita assured him there was nothing to fear. His food supply was nearly gone, but Tita chuckled with assurance that this was the last night he would need it, so why not cook it all?

"Tita, what IS this place?" Mujuni marveled as they nestled into the warmth of the hollowed tree for the night. "I don't mean the tree. I mean this valley. Where am I?"

"Ah, at last a question I can answer," Tita chuckled sleepily. "Let me tell you a story about this valley, and about our world. Perhaps you have heard some elements of truth in stories and songs. If you listen closely, you will hear it." And Tita began to hum, which is a delightful sensation in the dusk, in a tree trunk, when a boy's stomach is full and his eyelids heavy. Then Tita told a deeper story of the beginning of time.

Once upon a time when the world was young and rich in beauty, a people of great strength and goodness lived in Africa. Though evil had entered the hearts of humans, there were those who resisted its advance with determination and courage. Where other languages diverged and became unintelligible, these preserved the universal Language, the creative Word. Where others exploited the earth's provisions for personal gain, these strove to achieve harmony in their cultivation of crops and husbandry of animals. Where others sought spiritual power from fallen beings bent by evil in the service of Abaddon, these instead turned to worship the Creator alone, and only sought such help as the Creator in wisdom would offer.

Over generations these people continued to sing the story of the Universe, and pass down from father to son and mother to daughter the lessons they had learned. In their tradition there were many stories of visits by Messengers, in the form of powerful warriors or healers or poets, or sometimes all three. These Messengers were sent from the Creator. Most took the form of humans temporarily for their brief visits, delivering their prophecies or instructions, or using their strength to save a particular life or turn a particular battle. But some chose to incarnate themselves into the world by being born as actual animals in order to stay on earth for longer periods and truly enter into the struggle. They sought to preserve a remnant of people who resisted the advance of evil in the world. For the Creator wept over the choices of the people.

Gradually, from one century to another, as people increased in number and spread over all the continents, the scale of their evil and violence increased in proportion to their technological reach. When slave ships began to infest the shores of the continent, the faithful remnant sought a refuge where they could preserve their traditions. A Messenger came who led them to a valley, hidden in the mountains, where they established a Kingdom of sorts. There were some who would have stayed there forever, isolated from the world. But their leaders remembered that their purpose was not retreat and separation, but training for battle. For over five hundred years they have lived here now, immersed in a culture of learning, music, science, art, and plain hard work. Every generation some are sent out into the world, and some are brought in to learn and grow. Those sent out go with a task, a quest, a battle to fight, an idea to defend, a people to influence for good. But going out is always a risky business in this world, and loss and sorrow sometimes reverberate back into this valley.

Tita paused and then continued, "I am bringing you into this valley, and you must seek to know the specific way that only you can serve." Tita spoke to him gently as they lay down to sleep. "Tomorrow, my dear child, is the day. The day you have been waiting for all your life without really knowing it. You have learned much of who you are on this journey—a boy with courage, loyalty, a spirit of adventure, perseverance, a capacity for friendship, some wisdom. You have also learned your failings, and come to grief. Now you know your name. Tomorrow you find out who you really are."

Mujuni thought of the stone, and wondered if perhaps they would find some other document, or perhaps a wise old mukumu of some sort, a good sort perhaps, who hid in this valley and could answer his questions. Or maybe one of the messengers Tita had just spoken of. Having never been much more than an irritation or a useful servant at best to adults in his life, he felt some anxiety about meeting actual human beings the next day, if that was the plan. And some residual guilt that the death of Botu could not be justified by something so indulgent as him finding a stone that was a clue to his past. It would have been far better for the worthy dog to live on while he remained the ignorant Mu. As soon as these thoughts began to unsettle him, though, he found himself thinking instead of Birungi, Zowadi, and Nanjula, his cousins. He remembered their stories, their laughter, walking to school together, and he dared to hope that the end of his journey might include a similar sense of connection.

The morning dawned bright and fair. Now that he was rested, as he walked that morning Mujuni began to notice that some of the flowers he saw were completely different in color and shape from those on the other side of the mountains. Thus alerted, he looked closely at any bird he glimpsed flitting from branch to branch ahead on the path. Again the markings were unfamiliar, in spite of his month in the mountain range. In fact the entire atmosphere of this forest was different. The difference was hard to pinpoint exactly, less density to the understory, or a richer profusion of light from the canopy. He could only verbalize it as an absence of a sense of oppression. At first he attributed the difference to his own heart: walking freely with Tita instead of marching in a line of armed men. But with each passing hour he suspected it was more than that, a difference in the forest itself.

About noon they reached a clearing where they rested and drank from a clear stream. Mujuni had already removed his sweater, and now he removed the whole army uniform, stuffing it back into the pack and leaving on only his tattered, once-pink school shirt and shorts. The ground here was so warmed by the sun that he even decided to hang the shoes over the top of the pack and feel the earth with his feet, as he was accustomed. He was glad to be rid of the uniform of the rebels; it had been a useful protection up to this point, but in this peaceful place he did not want to be mistaken for a dangerous person. He noticed that Tita also had become livelier and livelier the farther they went on.

"Ahhh, the fragrance of home!" he nearly sang as they rested in the clearing.

"Is this your home, then?" Mujuni was surprised.

"On this earth, it is my home, let me put it that way." Tita was enigmatic as usual, but his good spirits were contagious. "Do you see that poinsettia tree ahead? Just on the edge of the clearing? That is the very place. You may place me back on the branch."

"Are we staying right here, then?" asked Mujuni. It seemed like a perfect spot, but then he was sharply reminded of Botu's absence. If only he could be here too! Mujuni felt the shame and loss keenly, perhaps even more so in this nearly ideal environment.

"Not we. I am staying here. You can manage the last few kilometers without me, the path from the clearing here is well marked."

"Without you? But I can't!" Mujuni felt panicked at the thought of leaving his guide and friend behind. The impending separation, combined with thoughts of Botu, made him ready to cry.

"Now, now, no one said you can't come back to visit me. I have been gone from my home for months now. And this chameleon body is not designed for the travels we have endured. I have told you everything I am permitted, and brought you as far as I needed to bring you. The last steps only you can take. But before we part, one gift has been permitted."

Tita whispered gently. "I can tell you one more chapter in your story. Botu was a messenger, a warrior. It was his choice to be born into this world's life as he was, and he did it to serve and protect you. He was a gift from your paternal grandparents, the puppy you remember in your dreams. We had thought him lost, but it was rumors of his reappearance some months ago that alerted us to your survival and location. He knew the risks; he knew this mortal life was a temporary form, and he accepted that for you. Your sorrow and grief are proper. But I did not want you to mourn him as one who has no hope. What you saw in life was only a temporal form of the true Botu. You killed him, yes, but he permitted it for your good. And you could kill only his earthly form. Do not grieve; it is time now to look ahead. Botu is a powerful friend still."

Mujuni slowly rose, holding the chameleon gently in his hand. Tita continued:

"I will wait here, in my tree, sleeping and sunning. If you haven't forgotten all about me by tomorrow then come back and visit."

"I would never, never forget you! Never." Mujuni was reassured by the promise of a meeting tomorrow. He gently placed the chameleon on a convenient branch. Though they had not been disturbed by any biting insects in the clearing, the poinsettia flowers were buzzing with fat pollinating flies. Mujuni supposed that was a chameleon heaven on earth. He smiled as he watched Tita's sticky tongue dart out and snag lunch.

A knot grew in Mujuni's stomach with each step along the path. The forest thinned into scattered trees and grassland. He began to notice signs of human presence: a clever bamboo water line carried pure mountain water down alongside the path; patches of cultivated gardens appeared, and stands of fruit trees grew among the bush. Below he could see the smoke of cooking fires.

The path turned and followed a ridge for a few hundred meters, then dipped down again. Now Mujuni could hear drums beating, and soon the sound of instruments, and voices

singing. He hesitated on the path, wondering if he was about to walk into a celebration of some sort where he would not be welcome. As he went on, slowly, he could see that flowers and fresh banana leaves had been tied to trees, a clear sign that this was a holiday, or that the people here were welcoming a visitor of some importance. The nagging doubt that he would be in the way almost made him run back to Tita's clearing.

But a healthy dose of curiosity kept him moving slowly onward. For one thing, he could not place the types of instruments he was hearing; their music was intriguing and new and inviting in some way. But more importantly, when the voices became clearer, he felt certain that a large proportion of them belonged to children. Again he realized how much he missed his cousins. The hope in his heart for a few friends finally overcame his hesitation. He reached outlying homes and did not pause, but kept a determined pace toward what sounded like the village center where all were gathered. He would later marvel over the stone and wood construction of the homes, the neat compounds, the artistic landscaping of flowers and trees, the clever devices for harnessing the sun's power, the fat dairy cows, and abundant hens. But that first afternoon, Mujuni was so determined to force himself onward that he hardly paused to consider his surroundings at all.

He finally reached the path's end. Never in his very best dreams could he have imagined what he saw there.

CHAPTER 21

The Quest Fulfilled

The center of the village featured a large garden—a grassy park ringed by tall spreading shade trees, clumps of bright yellow and orange lilies, marigolds, pink roses, and a dozen other varieties of flowers Mujuni had never seen. In the very center of the park was a thatched pavilion. Families sat on reed mats or small stools scattered comfortably in the shade all over the lawn, and most of the instruments and drums were scattered among them. The pavilion housed a number of singers and dancers, young men and women in bright matching dress. The men had rows of shells and bells tied around their ankles so that as they stamped their feet in time to the music they created a percussion counterpoint to their dance. A glistening muscular drummer seemed to lead the entire company from a massive waist-high drum in one corner, his arms raised high above his head then falling in a blur as he beat out the rhythm.

Seated on two carved wooden chairs in the center of the pavilion were a man and a woman, whom Mujuni supposed were the honored guests.

In an instant, he took in this scene, pausing at the border of the park to gaze around for a place to sit unnoticed and watch. But before he could move a step, everything began happening at once. The song changed and the dancers moved off the pavilion toward him. He wanted to back away, but a smiling boy started removing his backpack, and a very young girl held out a ring of flowers she clearly wanted to place over his head. Another girl was taking his hand and pulling him gently forward, toward the pavilion. By this time the dancers lined the path on each side, and the entire crowd had risen to its feet, singing. Children pressed in between the columns of dancers to run up and greet him, curious, shy, each murmuring some welcome and then falling in behind him.

There were four steps up to the raised platform of the pavilion, but when he stopped, the children behind him urged him on gently, with encouraging words and pats on the back. So he climbed up. The man had also risen from his seat; he seemed to be looking back at the woman and then at Mujuni, waiting. But as Mujuni's foot reached the top step the man sprang forward and threw his arms around him in a crushing hug. Mujuni was shocked, first to be hugged by the guest of honor, and secondly to realize that the man was crying, great shaking sobs racked his body for a long minute. Mujuni could not see his face thus engulfed, but he did not feel afraid.

At last the man released him a little. A hush had fallen over the entire crowd; even the children were silent, except for one crying baby. In the expectant quiet Mujuni saw that an older woman sat to the side of the pavilion, holding and patting a very fussy baby, whose whimpers seemed out of place in this otherwise amazing scene; Mujuni wondered for a moment why this baby was not given to its mother to feed, or taken away from the guests. But his attention was quickly drawn back to the man. Singing had resumed as the man went down on

one knee and began to carefully, slowly, unbutton Mujuni's tattered pink school shirt. The man helped him remove it, and then held out a beautiful shirt woven of an entire rainbow of colors, slipping it over Mujuni's head. The cotton felt soft, fresh, cool. When the shirt was on, the man hugged him again, at which point it dawned on Mujuni that the shirt matched the cloth of the man's clothes, and the woman's too.

Slowly the man rose, wiping his tears. Grasping Mujuni's hand firmly in his own, he led him solemnly to the chairs in the center. Now Mujuni was close enough to see that a third, empty, smaller chair had been placed between the man's and the woman's. And behind the chairs was a table decorated with flowers. In the center of the table he saw a cake, bigger than any he had ever imagined, covered with white icing and surrounded by roses. In the center of the cake, in a rainbow of icing colors, was written: "Welcome Home Mujuni."

From the moment his pack was removed to the moment he saw the cake, Mujuni had been led along as if in a dream. He was numb. The crowd he saw and heard as if through a glass, dimmed. He was certain at first that he had either stumbled into a party where he would soon be found out to be uninvited, not the person anticipated; or that he was being brought forward to be disciplined. He was completely overwhelmed by the man's greeting. Having been an orphan for as long as he could remember, he had no category to make sense of such treatment.

But seeing the chair, and his name on the cake, he suddenly awakened from his trance. A glimmer of hope sprang up in his heart.

All this time the woman had barely moved. She was not singing with the crowd, but sat staring, trembling faintly. Now
the man led Mujuni to the chair. He put the woman's hand in
Mujuni's, and Mujuni could feel that her palms were damp in
spite of her otherwise vacant stare. She was very thin, ill he
supposed, but beautiful, with smooth dark skin and braided
hair that rose in an intricate pile on her head. She put her
other hand on Mujuni's face, stroking his cheek.

"Mujuni?" she whispered.

Mujuni was never sure later what came over him, gave him
such confidence, but he slid out of his chair, knelt at her feet,
put his head in her lap while encircling her waist with his
arms.

"Mother, I'm home."

That was all he could manage to say.

EPILOGUE

One day, a few years before *Mujuni would come into this world, word came to the Mountain Kingdom that a people nearby, over their northwestern ridge, faced a great danger. A terrible disease known as Ebola had been mutated by Abaddon from its simian form into a viral particle that was infecting humans, causing them to bleed uncontrollably and die. People were in a panic. Dozens of deaths had occurred in two isolated villages in the vast Turini Rain Forest. Health workers were fleeing the entire area in fear, trade was arrested, the roads and borders were closed. Because the scholars of this Kingdom had researched many herbs over the generations, they had a preparation they believed could save lives in spite of the horrible virulence of this disease. The son of the aging King was widely acknowledged to be the most skilled in the art and science of healing. This young man was strong in Spirit as well as in body and mind. His name was Mugisa, blessing. He volunteered to go.*

And you know the story from there—how Mugisa served the people, how he fell in love with Zebiya, how her uncle the most powerful mukumu of the area allowed bitterness and jealousy to poison his heart further, how Mugisa and Zebiya hid away in the forest with their young son Mujuni until mother and infant were strong enough to journey to the valley. You know that Mugisa's parents had sent the puppy Botu as a gift for Mujuni on his first birthday.

The night before their planned departure, Zebiya placed Mujuni in a basket with Botu to keep him warm, as if she sensed the coming disaster. They awoke to the sounds of intruders. Mugisa struggled with the men in the darkness, but they were armed with guns. They shot both Mugisa and Zebiya and left them for dead, taking the baby, basket and all.

When Mugisa and Zebiya were revived after days of coma, they found themselves in a mission hospital far from the forest. Allies in the Kingdom's network had been informed of the attack within the hour by a crested eagle that roosted nearby. They came with stretchers and first aid, and managed to get the wounded couple to safety. Of course their first thought upon regaining consciousness was Mujuni, where was he, did he live. The hospital staff had investigated and learned that the baby was taken to the mukumu. There were rumors of human sacrifice being performed at this compound. The staff feared the worst. They decided to tell the couple that the baby had been found dead alongside them, and buried by the only home he had known, there in the forest. Mugisa and Zebiya grieved bitterly. About the time that they regained enough strength to travel, word came that Mugisa's father was dying, and they should come immediately. It was too dangerous to visit the baby's grave. They departed for the mountains with heavy hearts.

The people of the Kingdom embraced Mugisa and Zebiya as their new leaders upon the death of Mugisa's father. Though Zebiya loved her new home and though the people loved her, the wound in her heart never healed. She thought of Mujuni every day. Years passed. Mugisa's mother encouraged the couple to have another child, but Zebiya had been scarred so deeply, she feared to open her heart to the possibility. A decade passed. Then one day a Messenger came, one that only Zebiya saw. This messenger took the form of a chameleon, resting on a branch in her garden of flowers. He told her not to fear, to have another baby. This one would be a girl, and would be meant for the blessing of many people.

A few months later the people rejoiced to see their queen growing in girth; they whispered about her pregnancy and brought her gifts of fresh cream, ripe fruit, fish, eggs. But as the months wore on, her face became more and more pale and drawn. The growing child in her womb seemed to bring her nothing but memories of Mujuni. She ate less and less. Mugisa agonized over his wife's grief. The people prayed. They summoned musicians to lift her spirits. But in their hearts they knew that nothing short of Mujuni's return from the dead would lift the cloud that enveloped her soul.

She was nearing the end of her pregnancy when Mugisa received reports that a large yellow dog was haunting the villages of Zebiya's district, as if searching for something. By the time word reached the Kingdom of the dog and a boy being treated at the same mission hospital where Mugisa and Zebiya had been nursed to health, Zebiya was nearly ready to deliver. Mugisa dispatched a party of his warriors at once to bring them back, barely daring to hope that it could be Botu and never suspecting the identity of the boy. But they reached the sisters' clinic days after the boy and dog had disappeared. Though the trackers had great skill, the boy's trail disappeared at the river in the savannah. An elephant family had clearly walked there but migrated on toward the craters. They returned empty-handed the day that Zebiya delivered her daughter.

Over the next month Zebiya tried to care for her child, but her heart was not in it. Her milk came slowly and pitifully. The baby cried incessantly, hungry. Mugisa's mother tried to comfort her. The entire Kingdom worried over the health of mother and child. The situation looked desperate.

Then two days ago a leopard who patrolled the border reported that a boy had passed through the mountain's pass and was descending toward the valley. The leopard had spoken with a Messenger in the form of a chameleon named Tita while the boy bathed in the border river. He learned that Botu had found his ward at last, the boy was Mujuni, alive all these years in the home of the mukumu. Though Botu had been killed, the boy had survived, and was about to reach his destination. That night and all the next morning the Kingdom sprang to action preparing a great celebration. Only Mujuni could heal his mother's heart and save his sister, and now he was here, home at last—his quest as common and as glorious as merely to love and to be loved, now completed.

GLOSSARY

(Note: Italicized words are in the Luwendigo dialect)

abheka bhaliyo [translation] "How are those at home [i.e., your family]?"; part of a polite greeting sequence

acacia a type of tree, short and slender, with thorny branches and feather-like fronds of leaves; also, the illustrator of this book

Cape buffalo a heavy wild ox that roams in herds; lone males can be extremely dangerous

cassava a food crop (The starchy root may be roasted and eaten like a potato, or dried and pounded into flour called *kahunga* that is boiled in water to form a thin porridge or a thick, gelatinous carbohydrate meal. The green leaves may also be collected, chopped, and cooked into spinach-like greens.)

colobus any of a genus of long-tailed monkeys that travel the forest canopy, remarkable for their long, white fringes of fur

duiker a tiny forest antelope, the size of a small dog, with a rounded back and short legs

football soccer

fortnight two weeks

hartebeest a large species of antelope with a long, dark, narrow face and gently curving horns

jerry can a large square yellow plastic jug with a handle and spout, ubiquitous means of carrying water and fuel in places without pipelines; a full jerry can holds 20 liters (5 gallons) and weighs 20 kilograms (44 pounds)

kadobba a makeshift open lantern cut from a tin can (discarded food tins), filled with kerosene, and fitted with a wick

kahunga a type of flour, particularly the flour made from cassava root; also, the name of the dish when the flour is boiled into a thick gelatinous warm starch

kitengi a brightly patterned length of cotton cloth worn as a skirt wrapped around a woman's waist, or used as a blanket or scarf

kitubbi a grass thatch open-walled gazebo placed in front of a house; often the main meeting and greeting room on the compound

kob a small grass-eating gazelle that lives in herds on the savannah

liana a woody vine that hangs from trees in the tropical forest

Luwendigo the language of the Bawendigo people, living in the Rwendigo region

matoke a green cooking banana, like a plantain, that hangs from banana trees in heavy stalks (The thick skin must be peeled off with a knife, a tedious process because of a sticky sap that seeps out. Once boiled, it is mashed and eaten as a base for sauce.)

mbati corrugated tin sheets of roofing material which have supplanted traditional grass thatch as they are more water-proof and durable

mitwalo a unit of money worth ten thousand shillings, or five to ten dollars depending on the exchange rate

motocah a car, any motorized vehicle, as adopted from the English language

mpali biting ants; they often swarm and attach themselves to exposed skin

mukumu a type of priest in African traditional religion; someone who can intercede between humans and spirits; a mukumu may be hired to cast curses on others or provide protection from curses on oneself

mulimutya [translation] "How are you (plural)?"; part of a polite greeting sequence

mvuuli a tropical hardwood tree that grows to massive girth and height

mzee a term of respect for a man, roughly equivalent to "sir"; generally used to defer to an elder's age or experience

nightjar a bird active mostly at night, when it sits in the dust and waits for insects to rise up

obekekuni midges, tiny flies that swarm and bite, leaving an extremely itchy welt on most people

olayo [translation] "How was the night?"; a greeting used in the morning, or the first time encountering someone during the day; equivalent to "hello" in English

oribi a diminutive species of antelope with short spiky horns

panga machete

paraffin kerosene

petrol gasoline

posho cornmeal, ground maize

sisal a rough plant fiber, twisted into ropes

spoor animal track or scent, which may refer to its droppings

sufferia an aluminum cooking pan, deep and round with a lip of rim for holding on, but no handles

supu any sauce eaten over a starch, particularly the broth in a sauce of chicken or meat

tita father or uncle; the chameleon adopts this as his name

tugende [translation] "Let's go!"

tussock a low mound of thick grasses that clump together, providing footholds in areas that are otherwise swampy

ululate to wail or cry, in strong emotion, usually grief but sometimes in celebration as well; a loud singsong expression

umbrella tree colloquial name for a tropical tree with a wide canopy providing ample shade; popular location for schools, clubs, and community gatherings

waterbuck a large antelope with a thick oily fur, which looks like a reindeer and is found near water

wattle a grid of sticks and reeds that is a skeleton for constructing homes; mud is added to the mesh to form a solid wall

ACKNOWLEDGMENTS

This book was written in late-night moments (solar power permitting) in a mud-brick house in a remote village, while juggling life as a mom of four kids and a doctor running nutrition programs and treating malaria. I wanted to give my kids a gift for Christmas, and as they were avid readers but had no books that talked about their world, I decided to write one myself. We read the first chapter on Christmas Eve, sitting in the dark around our tree, which was a glorified branch cut from the abundant jungle of our yard. And so a tradition was born, which continued through four holidays, a loosely connected series of novels in which capital-T Truth was embodied in contemporary stories from their world.

My first and main thanks goes to Jack, Julia, Caleb, and Luke for listening, for reading, for clamoring for more. You are my audience. This is for you. This first book is particularly dedicated to Jack, about whom we often said that he and our yellow Labrador named Star were one soul in two bodies. Jack inhales words, and has the same spirit of courage and curiosity that would propel a boy to brave hyenas and soldiers, and save the life of his sister.

As much as I love to write, and love my kids, nothing would have happened without the unwavering support of my husband, Scott, who gave me the space to complete this book by shouldering every problem of our life from patient emergencies to insect invasions. He is my partner and friend in every aspect of life, this one included, my first reader and my true love.

Acacia Masso grew up with us, as her parents were on our team. After my own kids, hers was the next family to read the books. For three years she actually lived in our home. So when New Growth Press expressed interest in publishing, I sent them some of Acacia's artwork anonymously to see if they would be interested. Thankfully they saw her talent. What a gift to have an illustrator who knows just what everything should look like, because she lived the stories too!

New Growth Press made the journey from an informal, personal, family story to a publishable novel blessedly smooth. Thanks to Patric Knaak who introduced me to Barbara Juliani over a lunch meeting. and to Barbara who asked to read the books I had written for my kids. Her belief in the stories gave them a new life I never expected, a decade after they were written. Nancy Winter clarified and improved my prose. Tim Green and the Faceout Studio team created the perfect cover and artistic layout. Cheryl White has been kind and patient with my complete inexperience as an author, and along with Michele Walton and Gretchen Logterman, has done the nitty-gritty work of making this a real book and getting it into real hands.

Lastly, I want to thank my mom, Judy Aylestock, whose love for books poured over into my own heart and whose impeccable English made me a better writer. She was this book's final editor, and will probably be its biggest promoter.

Soli Deo gloria.

READ ON FOR A SNEAK PEAK AT BOOK 2

OF *THE RWENDIGO TALES*

A Bird, a Girl, and a Rescue

The rain swept in from the north as Kiisa and her father, Mugisa, reached the school. Mugisa pulled the admission letter from his satchel, and the gatekeeper waved them in. They nearly ran across the football field as gray clouds began to hurl the first heavy drops of cold water on their heads. Thunder rumbled, adding to the impression of an approaching force. Kiisa shivered as they finally reached the shelter of the administration porch, just as the drops consolidated into sheets of powerful water. The *mbati* roof magnified the percussion of the rain, enveloping them in a cocoon of pounding noise. She moved closer to her father. Even the equatorial jungle could be cool in a rain like this one. They watched older students pull clothes off the fences where their laundry had been draped and scurry into their dorms.

Finally, the rain tapered off into mist. Mugisa cleared his throat politely, since they had not been noticed by the secretary; she seemed to be asleep with her head bent down on the reception desk, a plain wooden table just inside the door. She looked up sleepily, surprised at their appearance. Unlike most prospective parents, the man before her did not look at all intimidated by the surroundings of school and office. In fact, he looked regal, dressed in a colorful woven cloth not traditional in that area, and he stood taller than most of the local tribe. The girl beside him, however, seemed to be trying to disappear under his arm, shivering more than could be explained by the coolness of the afternoon rain.

"Ahem, *olayo*," he began in a proper greeting.

"*Olayo*," she replied, fully awake now and curious, as the clarity of his local dialect clashed with the hint of the foreign in his dress and manner.

"I have come to bring my daughter to enroll in the Senior One class."

"Of course, of course, please have a seat on the form just inside the door. The headmaster is not yet back from lunch."

Slowly the school began to emerge once more from the mist as Kiisa and her father sat waiting. They saw neat gravel paths criss-crossing a grassy square whose perimeter consisted of low white-limed buildings with matching blue *mbati* roofs. Students in uniforms of drab gray skirts or pants with neatly pressed white shirts emerged from the doors when a bell rang, but within five minutes the schoolyard emptied again. Kiisa noted smoke rising from somewhere behind the classes, down a hill perhaps, and wondered what kind of food would be offered. Kiisa had a healthy appetite, and food was one of her greatest anxieties about the whole boarding school plan.

Just as she had begun to think of steaming fresh milk from the cow at home mixed with sugar from canes in the valley and a bit of cocoa dried and pounded from trees on the hillside . . . her daydream was abruptly ended by her father standing and gently leading her by the hand into the Headmaster's office. There a surprisingly small man sat behind a surprisingly large desk. He stood to shake hands with Mugisa, who then handed Kiisa's admission letter to him for inspection. Kiisa did not listen very carefully to the entire proceeding. She was vaguely aware that the Headmaster seemed familiar with her father, and she supposed that may have been from Mugisa's work in the district more than a decade before she was born, when he met and married her mother. The stories she had heard from that time made her curious, but fearful. Her older brother, Mujuni, had not been sent back here for schooling, and at twenty-one he was already nearly finished with the five years of University instruction that would qualify him as a medical doctor in the capital city. But Kiisa's parents felt that she needed some exposure to her mother's culture, and that she was ready for the challenge of boarding school. Kiisa was far from convinced. . . .

AFRICAN REBELS. STOLEN GIRLS.
ILLEGAL LOGGING. A DANGEROUS COBRA.

Join eleven-year-old Kiisa and her messenger bird, Njili, on a thrilling rescue mission in the second page-turning book in J. A. Myhre's adventure fiction series for kids and young adults, *The Rwendigo Tales*.

Read a Story, Change a Story

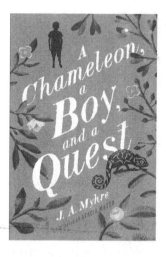 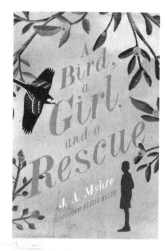

Thank you for reading the Rwendigo Tales. Though they are fictional stories, the events and characters have roots in a real place near the center of the African continent.

The author donates half of her royalties to a fund that enables real children to emerge with resilience from childhoods threatened by poverty, rebel warfare, human trafficking, malnutrition, loss, and fear.

Your purchase of this book enables orphans to receive an education, babies of HIV-positive mothers to receive food, children who have never held a book to receive a library, and much more. These small acts of justice and mercy have the power to bring hope and enable communities to write new endings to their own stories.

For more information, or to make a donation to the Rwendigo Fund, which supports the work described above, please visit serge.org/hope.

To discover more Serge publications, please visit serge.org/resources.

www.newgrowthpress.com

Grace at the Fray